CHRISTMAS ON CRUMCAREY

BETH RAIN

Copyright © 2022 by Beth Rain

Christmas on Crumcarey by Beth Rain

First Publication: 9th December, 2022

All rights reserved.

No part of this book may be reproduced in any form or by any electronic or mechanical means, including information storage and retrieval systems. Except for use in any review, the reproduction or utilization of this work, in whole or in part, in any form by any electronic, mechanical or other means now known or hereafter invented, is forbidden without the written permission of the publisher.

Published by Beth Rain. The author may be contacted by email on bethrainauthor@gmail.com

❀ Created with Vellum

CHAPTER 1

*I*vy Evans wriggled in the passenger seat, trying to get comfortable. Her breath was leaving little foggy clouds in the air in front of her, but she resisted the siren call of the heater switch. The last time she'd given it a prod – about five hours ago - Gareth had whined that the warm air was making him sleepy.

Ivy let out a sigh. She was cold, stiff and cramped – but what else could she expect? It was the day before Christmas Eve after all, and they'd been on the road for almost eight hours. Her tiny car wasn't made for epic adventures like this trek all the way from Somerset to Scotland. Still – it would be worth it, wouldn't it? It wasn't every day a girl was whisked away by a gorgeous man for Christmas!

Wrapping her arms around herself in an attempt to warm up, Ivy tried to ignore the fact that the seatbelt had started to rub against her neck. She was bored. She hated being a passenger – she'd have much preferred to share some of the driving. Unfortunately, Gareth had other ideas. In fact, he'd become decidedly stroppy about the whole thing when she'd offered to take over for a few hours.

Still, she knew she should be grateful. She was sure Gareth was just being a gentleman and trying to get their trip off to a good start. That said, if she'd been allowed to drive for a bit, they could have at least turned the heating on – she didn't find being nice and warm at all distracting. Plus, singing along to a few Christmas tunes on the radio would have made the miles fly by.

Unfortunately, Gareth *didn't* like driving with music on. Instead, he'd insisted on tuning into a turgid talk about conceptual art that had managed to make forty-five minutes last an entire lifetime – or that's how it had felt to Ivy. If the presenter had said "juxtaposition" one more time, she'd have screamed.

Ah well - they were nearly there now.

Ivy felt her heart give an excited flip. This was it - after two years together... well, *almost* two years... Gareth was finally going to pop the question. At least, Ivy was pretty sure that's what he was planning. After all – he'd *said* that he had something important to ask her when they got there... and what else could this romantic getaway be about?

If she was being completely honest, Ivy couldn't

quite believe that Gareth had arranged it all – it was just so unlike him! A cosy, Christmas escape to a beautiful cottage right on the shores of a Scottish loch… Ivy couldn't believe her luck. It was so romantic!

As if the cottage wasn't enough of a treat, Gareth had also surprised her with an early Christmas present - tickets for a "there and back again" flight over to Crumcarey Island. Ivy had never heard of the place before, but the handful of photographs she'd managed to find online were stunning. According to Gareth, it was the eighth shortest flight in the world – lasting just a couple of minutes from take-off to landing.

Ivy couldn't imagine asking for a present like this in her wildest dreams, but now that she'd had the chance to get used to the idea, she could see that it could be a lot of fun. They were booked onto the special festive flight in the morning, and then they'd be back by lunchtime – ready to enjoy the rest of Christmas Eve in their gorgeous cottage. With any luck, they'd be able to get some cute "newly engaged" photographs while they were there too!

The words "newly engaged" seemed to echo around her as though they were bouncing off the mountains that loomed in the distance. The rugged scenery had been breathtaking as they'd meandered their way up through Scotland. Now – at just twenty to four in the afternoon - the sun was already getting ready to dive behind the horizon and everything was starting to look a bit sinister and shadowy out there.

Ivy sighed and wriggled again.

'Will you quit it!' snapped Gareth. 'I'm trying to concentrate here!'

'Sorry,' she said, turning to smile at him. 'I'm just excited.'

'Oh,' said Gareth, staring dead ahead, his hands firmly in the eleven and two positions on the wheel. 'Well – yeah, I guess you should be!'

Working hard to contain an eye roll as a self-satisfied look spread across Gareth's face, Ivy stared at him. Her future *husband*? She shivered slightly.

Gareth was still just as handsome as the first day she'd spotted him across a crowded student bar - well-groomed and chisel cheeked. She'd been busy gate-crashing the local student union with a group of friends who'd decided that she was due a much-needed night out. Several shots of tequila later, Ivy had ended up approaching Gareth on a dare.

Her friends had been on a mission to push her out of her comfort zone - the group consensus was that she'd been single for far too long. Ivy had always been a planner. It made her an excellent virtual PA to the various estate agents she worked for – but not so great when it came to inviting change into her life in the shape of handsome strangers.

Now here she was, eighteen months later, and that same handsome stranger was whisking her off to Scotland to propose.

Ivy quickly turned to stare back out of the window.

If she carried on watching Gareth, she was going to end up asking him how and when he was planning to do it – and that would spoil everything. This was the problem with hating surprises. She wanted to be prepared for every eventuality in life – but it did take some of the wonder out of the truly special moments. She'd already managed to extract the details of the trip from him so that she could research everything thoroughly online.

Ivy started to let out another sigh, but promptly cut herself off when she caught him shooting her an annoyed glance. She chewed her lip as irritation flared in her chest. It was never very far from the surface these days… but now wasn't the time to let it out. Ivy was determined that this trip was going to make everything right between them again. Somehow.

She had to admit it - they'd been going through a… sticky patch. Even Gareth had noticed something was up – and that took some doing. Then, just as she'd been starting to wonder if they really had much of a future together, he'd changed everything by telling her that he had something important to ask her. It had given Ivy something to cling to. She was hoping it was a sign that - if something was *really* important - Gareth could pull out all the stops. It certainly wasn't something that happened very often.

The problem was – she found Gareth incredibly difficult to live with. Ivy was sure it was the size of her flat that was the problem. Or at least - she was hoping that was the case. The place was minuscule. It had been perfect when it was just her, but the pair of them just didn't seem to fit somehow. Perhaps a bit more space would stop the constant tension between them.

That said, while she was still paying the vast majority of the rent, as well as coughing up for all the bills and food, she wasn't *that* keen on moving to a larger and more expensive place. Of course, it would help if Gareth started paying his half of everything – but his view on the matter was that it was *her* flat – he was just staying there for a bit, so why should he help towards the rent?

She'd been so excited when Gareth had asked if he could move in with her when he'd come to the end of his degree. He'd assured her that it would only be a temporary thing until he got himself a new job and could find his own place. At the time, she'd been over the moon to have the chance to "play house" with her gorgeous boyfriend. Unfortunately, it was now a year later and the thrill of living together had worn so thin it was practically threadbare.

Ivy thought it was because Gareth had never had to look after himself. He'd chosen his degree in Art History at the local university because it meant he'd been able to continue living with his parents. So - his long-suffering mother had carried on cooking for him, cleaning up after him and ironing his underpants – for an extra three years. Ivy had the sneaking suspicion that it was his mum who'd suggested that he moved into her flat. Perhaps she'd had enough of playing nursemaid to her adult son!

Despite his love of over-using words like juxtaposition, avant-garde, and contextualisation, Gareth had somehow managed to fail all his exams and graduate without honours. Eventually, he'd found himself an entry-level role working in telemarketing - where Ivy was pretty sure he didn't get to use juxtaposed in any of his scripts. It seemed like he was always in the running for a promotion, but every time he was overtaken at the last minute by someone who'd only just joined the company.

There was definitely a pattern in there somewhere, but Ivy couldn't quite figure out what it was. Either Gareth was being unfairly held back, or he was just truly crap at his job.

Either way, maybe getting around to asking her to marry him would be the beginning of a whole new Gareth. Ivy bit her lip, doing her best to ignore the fact that she really didn't believe in such things. In her experience, people didn't change – not really – not deep down where it mattered.

Still, she had to hope that there was a chance that living with her was starting to rub off on him. Perhaps he really *was* ready to grow up a bit. Maybe he'd finally iron his own underpants for a change. Sure, it had taken a bit longer than was ideal – but she had to admit, she was probably not the easiest person to live with either.

Ivy liked things a certain way, and suddenly finding herself living with a man-child had been… challenging. She'd adored him of course… at least she had when he'd first moved in and everything was so fresh and exciting, but now… there were definitely doubts lurking somewhere deep down.

Ironically, these doubts were fuelled by the same group of friends who'd dared her to go up to Gareth in the first place. They'd all labelled him a "total prat" … and sometimes a lot worse than that – but Ivy wasn't one to give up on things without a fight.

When he proposed, all these petty problems were bound to melt away, weren't they? Now they were driving north, and she was determined that this Christmas together in their cosy cottage was going to change everything for them.

Ivy frowned out of the window as she imagined Gareth getting down on one knee in front of the flickering flames of an open fire, as Christmas songs crooned from a vintage radio. Maybe there would even be mulled wine and mince pies on a tartan rug.

She felt the little squirm in her stomach again… that feeling she'd been busy trying to convince herself for the past eight hours was excitement. All of a sudden, she had to wonder if it might actually be pure dread instead.

Ivy blinked and pushed the thought to the back of her mind, distracted by the scene unfolding outside.

Huh, that was odd!

If they were almost at the gorgeous, cosy cottage, why were there signs out there letting them know that they were nearly at an airport? And why had Gareth just started indicating? Was this all a part of the surprise?

'Are we stopping?' she asked, her voice faint as her heart gave a squeeze. She knew that feeling - it was getting ready to plummet. They were now following a stretch of chain-link fence topped with razor wire. In front of them, getting closer by the second, was a grotty motel with a small airport building and runway just behind it.

Gareth pulled into a parking space in front of the squat, ugly brick building. Ivy stared at the filthy windows with their grubby, yellowing net curtains.

What were they doing here? And where was her cosy cottage?

CHAPTER 2

'*H*ahaha!'

The laugh burst out of Ivy. She was tired, but she owed it to Gareth to laugh at his joke - even if it was in pretty bad taste. After so many hours in the car, the least she could do was fake-appreciate his attempt at humour. 'Haha!' she added. 'I really thought you meant it!'

'I don't see what's so funny,' said Gareth, killing the engine and her mood at the same time. He turned to her with what Ivy always thought of as his *pious* face.

'You - saying that we're staying here!' said Ivy. Her laugh had just withered like a limp *you-know-what*. She was still smiling, but it was flickering on and off like a fluorescent strip light on its last legs.

'We *are* staying here,' huffed Gareth. 'You're not disappointed, are you?'

Disappointed?!

Ivy didn't have a rude enough word in her vocabulary to tell him how disappointed she was right now. Not that it mattered in the slightest anyway, because he didn't actually pause for any kind of response.

'It's only a room, Ivy,' he huffed. 'It's cheaper and closer to the airport for your treat, so don't sulk.'

Ivy bit her tongue. She hated it when he accused her of sulking. It was like some kind of self-fulfilling prophecy. He accused her of it, and she promptly started to sulk. It had become his favourite way of getting under her skin recently.

It was even worse because it was true. Ivy hated to admit it, but she tended to end up in some kind of sulk at least once a day… it was probably the thing she hated most about herself. She couldn't remember being this bad before Gareth had moved in with her… but then, maybe that was just because there had been no one close enough to her who was willing to point it out.

Ivy stared out at the motel. Nope, no matter how hard she stared at it, it wasn't turning into a beautiful, cosy cottage with a hot tub on the deck and an open fire and candles everywhere.

Gareth was staring ahead too, looking like she'd mortally wounded him.

'Fine,' she sighed.

'You're so ungrateful sometimes, you know,' he huffed. 'I just drove nine hours straight just so you could go on this flight.'

Ivy frowned. That was *spectacularly* unfair. This whole thing had been his idea – from the cosy cottage to the quick trip to Crumcarey. She'd never once mentioned to Gareth that she even *wanted* to experience the eighth shortest flight in the world. She hadn't even contemplated the existence of such a thing before he'd mentioned it.

'Come on,' she sighed. 'Let's go in.'

'You could sound a bit more enthusiastic after all the effort I've put in.'

Ivy was going to end up biting through her tongue at this rate if he kept up the martyr act. Still, they *had* just driven all this way together, and she couldn't stay in the car indefinitely. Anyway, she needed a pee.

Yanking the door open, Ivy's arm was nearly ripped out of its socket by the wind. She hurried out of her seat, wrestling against the elements until she managed to force the car door closed by throwing her entire body weight against it.

'Bloody hell!' she laughed, the sound shocked out of her by the fact that she could barely keep herself upright - her feet planted wide apart as the wind whipped long strands of dark hair madly around her face.

'Are you going to help with the bags or what?!' demanded Gareth.

The unexpected rush of mad-weather-joy drained straight out of her. She marched to the open boot, grabbed her old rucksack and turned to head for the motel, leaving Gareth to fend for himself.

Pushing against the smeared glass of the double doors, Ivy felt her heart plummet further. She'd had some vague hope that the place might prove to be nicer inside than outside. Perhaps it would be one of those hidden gems people were always going on about.

Huh – no such luck.

With every step she took towards the reception desk, she felt the sticky suction of the soles of her trainers as they struggled to peel away from the grime covering the orange and brown swirly carpet.

Eew! This definitely didn't bode well for the state of their room!

'Erm, hi!' she said to the guy at the reception desk. He was sitting behind a decidedly unfriendly-looking glass barrier that made the whole place feel a lot more like she was signing in at a prison than a hotel.

The man didn't look up from the old-fashioned, boxy monitor in front of him. Ivy cleared her throat - but there was still no reaction. Doing her best to swallow down the bubbling irritation that was rapidly transforming into a burgeoning temper tantrum, Ivy knocked sharply on the glass.

'What?' came the response.

Ivy's eyebrows shot up. Clearly, the customer service here matched the décor. But no, she needed to give the poor guy the benefit of the doubt... even if he *had* just started exploring the contents of his left nostril with his little finger.

'We've got a room booked,' said Ivy, staring hard at the counter in front of her – anything to save her from having to watch him either lick or flick his nostril findings. Frankly – she didn't want that image burned into her brain!

'Name?' demanded the man in a bored tone.

'Erm – it's probably under Gareth Pugh,' she said.

The guy glanced down at a piece of paper.

'Nope. No Gareth Pugh.'

Ivy frowned. She should have waited for Gareth, shouldn't she?! Ooh, what if he'd done something insanely cute and put it under her soon-to-be Mrs Pugh name?!

'Try Ivy Pugh?' said Ivy, unable to stop a tiny smile from flickering its way through her bad mood.

'Nope,' said the guy again.

Ivy's shoulders dropped.

'We go by credit card names,' he said. 'I've got an Ivy here – but not Pugh.'

'Evans?' said Ivy.

'Yeah! There you are,' he said. 'See – that wasn't so hard, was it?!'

Ivy did her best not to let out a growl, but by the look of mild terror the man was now throwing at her, she guessed she wasn't doing such a great job.

'First floor. Here's your key,' he muttered.

'Great,' said Ivy, her voice completely flat as the guy

plonked a massive plastic baton onto the desk in front of him and then slid open a hatch so that she could reach through for it.

Resisting the urge to pull the cuff of her jumper down so that she didn't actually have to touch the key with her bare fingers, she picked it up with a slight shudder.

Turning away from the reception desk so that she didn't have to watch the man's resumed nostril-foraging, Ivy paused for a second. Should she wait for Gareth before heading up to the room? No, maybe not… for his own safety.

Ivy felt like she needed two seconds on her own. It was going to take some serious deep breathing to get herself under control. It was bad enough that she was going to be spending Christmas in this shithole instead of the cottage she'd been obsessing over to the point of using its picture as her laptop screensaver. Add in the fact that Gareth had used *her* credit card to pay for it, and she was in danger of going supernova!

Turning towards the lift, Ivy came face to face with a dog-eared scrap of paper with the words "Out Of Odour" scrawled on it. Resisting the urge to get a pen out of her handbag to correct the spelling, she turned and took the stairs at a jog.

The burst of exercise felt unexpectedly good after being cooped up in the car for so long. That was the only reason she was feeling quite so miffed, wasn't it?

She was just overreacting. Maybe after a couple of moments to herself, she'd see the funny side of all this.

Letting herself into room twelve, Ivy didn't give herself a second to look around before pelting towards the door for the ensuite. Yanking it open, she came face to face with a wall of shelves with a couple of desultory, stained-looking pillows.

'What?!' she gasped, crossing her legs. There wasn't another door in here. Didn't they even have their own loo?

Muttering under her breath, Ivy shot back out into the hallway not bothering to lock the door behind her and scuttled along the corridor until she found what she was looking for.

Two minutes later, after practically taking the entire top layer of skin off her hands with the industrial-grade liquid soap on the edge of the grotty sink, Ivy dragged her feet back towards the room.

'You could have bloody waited for me!'

Gareth was sitting on one of the twin beds and he was doing an excellent impression of a sulky toddler.

'Sorry, Gar,' she sighed. 'I was desperate!'

'You're developing an old lady bladder, you know,' he huffed.

Ivy felt her fingers twitch as if they were independently itching to wrap themselves around his neck. She flexed them quickly, turning to fiddle with her rucksack until she could be sure she wasn't pulling a murder-face.

This wasn't how this trip was meant to start. After all, they'd driven all this way. Ivy had been so desperately hoping that this Christmas would give them both the clean slate they needed. She didn't want to be the one to ruin it just because she was tired and a bit disappointed.

Ivy quickly plastered a smile onto her face and made the snap decision not to mention the whole credit-card thing for now - at least until she'd calmed down a bit.

Staring at the bedspread Gareth was sitting on, she couldn't help but wrinkle her nose. She wanted to sink down next to him and feel his arms wrap around her. Then maybe they could both laugh about all this... but that bedspread made her pause. The swirling, seventies pattern could well be hiding a multitude of sins.

Grabbing her coat, she laid it on the bed opposite Gareth and sat down. There – no direct contact and she could always pop the coat in the wash when they got back.

Ivy shot Gareth a tight smile, hoping to ease the weird atmosphere between them, but he was too busy fiddling with his shoelaces to notice. She tried to let the tension go from her shoulders and took a second to stare around the room – hoping that maybe it wasn't *quite* as bad as her first impression.

Drab and Dusty – both with a very purposeful capital D. Clearly this place didn't set much store in deep cleaning. Add in the clashing 1970s patterns on the carpet and dodgy bedspreads, and it all came together in a way that set her head spinning. Gareth really had better get on with getting down on one knee before the motifs on the curtains juxtaposed with the pattern of the carpet and gave them both a headache!

GAH! That blasted word! That up-its-own-bum art show he'd forced her to listen to in the car had sunk in further than she'd realised. Ivy quickly made a silent vow never to say – or even *think* – the word "juxtaposition" ever again.

Maybe... maybe if Gareth got on and asked her, she'd be able to use the rush of blissed-out happiness to convince him that the cosy cottage really *was* a better bet than staying here. She wouldn't mind adding it to her credit card – hell, she'd wring its little plastic neck for every penny if it meant they could escape this place. She wasn't looking forward to testing out the rather dubious comforts of this single bed. There was no chance she'd get much sleep on this thing – and not for any fun, bouncy-bouncy newly-engaged reasons either!

Suddenly, Ivy felt like she was in the middle of a very weird dream. Maybe if she gave herself a little pinch, she'd wake up in the car and Gareth would tell her that they were nearly at the cottage.

She shot a glance at Gareth, who was now watching her uneasily. Hmm – maybe she'd better not pinch herself after all. He was doing that thing where he was running his tongue along his front teeth – a sure sign he was brewing up to say something and had the words all prepared.

Gareth wasn't great with words. As a telemarketer, he usually had a script in front of him and never had to figure anything out for himself other than remembering to ask people for their credit card details before the end of the call. According to his boss, Gareth regularly forgot that bit. Maybe that's why he never got promoted!

Ivy could see that Gareth was already struggling to line his words up. Poor thing – she should cut him some slack really. This whole proposing lark was going to be a bit of a challenge – he had to remember what to say and how he was going to say it. Ivy watched his face in fascination – it looked like the whole thing was causing him considerable pain.

If only it was the done thing for her to offer him a few tips… "My beautiful Ivy" would be a fairly good start, or maybe "I love you more than words can say and I will learn how to make my own bed" – though, to be fair, that might be pushing it a bit.

Gareth opened his mouth and Ivy blinked, doing her best to drag her thoughts back to the present moment. After all, she didn't want to miss actually hearing it because she was too busy with her own scenarios.

'Ivy,' he said, his face serious, 'I think it's time we moved our relationship on to the next step.'

Okay – so not exactly ten out of ten on the romance

stakes, and there was no hint of a knee-bend just yet. All in all, it was a fairly average start but at least it was going in the right direction.

'I know it's a big commitment,' he said, 'but I'm ready for it.'

Still not dripping with romance - but Gareth had just reached out and taken her hand, which added a nice touch.

Ivy met his eyes, and she had to force down a giggle as Gareth stared meaningfully back at her. This was it, wasn't it? He was going to ask her!

'Ivy,' he said, swallowing nervously, 'I think we should get a dog.'

CHAPTER 3

*I*t had been the most awkward night in the history of awkward nights.

Ever.

Ever ever ever.

Ivy knocked her forehead lightly against the tiny round portal window of the even tinier plane. She couldn't quite fathom how she'd ended up in this state on Christmas Eve. She'd never felt less festive in her entire life.

'Merrily on high, my arse!' she muttered, huffing up the window.

Not only was she sitting here, waiting for her turn on the eighth shortest flight in the world without her fiancé… she didn't even *have* a fiancé!

'He wants a bloody… effing… dog?!' she fumed.

Ivy wasn't worried about disturbing anyone, because right now she was the only person on board.

The pilot was still standing outside on the tarmac waiting for the other passengers to appear. She guessed she really should have told him that Gareth was too busy sulking to come... but she didn't feel like making excuses for him right now.

Ivy checked her phone. Yup, it was official – they were running late. According to the times printed on the leaflet that had been in the envelope with her ticket, they should already be in the air by now. But if they were talking about *should* here – she *should* be engaged, and her fiancé *should* be sitting right next to her. Instead, she was here on her own and Gareth was back in the motel nursing a particularly bad mood.

Ivy couldn't believe that Gareth had dared to lose his temper with her just because she still wanted to take the trip to Crumcarey. Especially considering the fact that she'd been tricked into coming all this way by the promise of romance in a cosy cottage that had never materialised. He'd expected her to stay in the room with him and "talk things through". The nerve of the man!

Ivy didn't know why he was so bothered about her taking some time out. He'd been giving her the cold shoulder ever since they'd woken up. *Quite frankly,* the peace and quiet had been a bit of a relief. Gareth's voice had cut through the fuggy air of their horrible room late into the night as he'd monologued on the various responsibilities of being Good Dog Owners.

Sometime around three in the morning - just as Ivy

was enjoying the distraction of a spring doing its best to drill a hole in her back - Gareth had started on the less-than-fascinating topic of drawing up a walking schedule. Then he'd announced that it would be best if she did the early morning walks. Ivy had just grunted, willing him to shut up and leave her to be tortured by the bed in peace. Sadly, it hadn't worked out that way.

"You know how I like to have the kitchen to myself in the mornings without you getting in my way. Having breakfast in peace is vital to my mental well-being – and having a dog will help with that if you're out walking it."

As the words replayed in her head, Ivy realised she was grinding her teeth - and quickly forced herself to stop. The last thing she needed was to give herself lockjaw! Noticing that her hands were tightly clenched into fists in her lap, she flexed her fingers, doing her best to let some of the tension go.

But... it was *her* flat for goodness sake. This feeling of constantly being in the way was becoming worryingly familiar. That couldn't be right, could it?!

She pulled in a deep breath and let it out slowly, trying to channel the wonderfully zen woman on her meditation app. She managed to count to four before giving it up for a bad job - the voice in her head was spitting the numbers out as though they were poisoned eggnog.

Hmm... zen not quite achieved this time!

Ivy was just tired – that was all. No prizes for guessing why that was! At around five in the morning -

just as she'd finally started to drift off - Gareth had snatched away the tantalising taste of sleep by telling her that she could buy some air fresheners if she was worried about the smell of dog getting on the furniture.

That was the point she'd asked him to *pretty please* let her get some sleep. Okay – so, that wasn't what she'd said at all. What she'd *actually* said was so rude that thinking about it now made her blush. Still – even that hadn't done the trick. There had been a three-second pause... just enough to get her hopes up... and then off he went again.

"Fine. I'll do my best not to let it onto the sofa – but it is going to happen sometimes - muddy paws or not. It's just part of having a dog, Ivy."

Ivy knew that – of course she did. But at five in the morning, she simply hadn't had the energy to point out that this particular sofa belonged to her – not him. She'd paid for it. As usual, Gareth had said he'd pay half and then, mysteriously, the cash never materialised.

'Knobhead,' she muttered to the still-empty plane.

Because... well... that sort of thing seemed to happen a lot. Whenever Ivy made the mistake of asking him for a contribution, she was always met with a scathing response. According to Gareth, he did enough around the place, and the financial side of things was her responsibility.

Other than the few times he'd taken the bins out, Ivy struggled to think of much Gareth did to help. In a way, she wished he wouldn't even bother with that - because he'd be moody about it for days afterwards and complain endlessly. His mother really had created a monster.

Ivy turned back to the portal window and took another deep breath as she watched the pilot check his watch. Perhaps this trip to a motel in the middle of nowhere *was* going to change her life after all – just not in the way she'd been expecting.

If only Gareth had agreed to come, maybe they could have talked things through and cleared the air. Instead, here she was – off on her own on Christmas Eve while he sat on one of the most uncomfortable beds in the universe, stewing in his own juices. Well, it served him right.

She'd be back in an hour... maybe he'd be in a better mood by then. Ivy really hoped so, otherwise she was going to go off in search of that cottage all on her own!

Suddenly, a movement outside on the runway caught her attention. Ivy craned her neck as she watched someone running across the tarmac towards the pilot. For a moment, she thought it might be Gareth - changing his mind and dashing to be at her side.

Fat chance!

It was just one of the airport ground crew wearing a very soggy Santa hat. After a few words in the pilot's ear, he turned tail and ran back towards the airport building.

'Right!' said the pilot, appearing as if by magic at the top of the steps and smiling at her. 'So sorry for the delay. I've just been told that the rest of the passengers aren't coming after all. Well – all but one of them are accounted for...'

'Oh,' said Ivy. Now she *really* couldn't mention Gareth without looking like a thoughtless idiot.

'Yeah,' he said with a shrug. 'Stag party. They've rather... overdone it? Apparently, they're all still a bit... tired?'

Ivy smirked. That was clearly a polite way of saying they were all too busy hugging their toilet bowls – probably just down the corridor from where she'd left Gareth in his K9-induced sulk.

'It might be just a short hop to Crumcarey, but it's often more than the stag parties can handle when it comes down to it!' said the pilot cheerfully. He pulled the door closed with a clonk and squeezed into his seat. 'Makes no difference to us, though – they've paid in advance and the fare's non-refundable. We learned to do that the hard way!'

Ivy grinned. What a bunch of idiots! Now that she was here, she realised she wouldn't miss this for the world... a whole hour of peace and quiet... bliss!

'As for the other chap who's missing,' continued the pilot, 'according to Jane in the office, that was one of the complimentary tickets we sent out to an insurance company. It's pretty rare those get used so I'm not too concerned about that particular no-show!'

The pilot turned back to the console and started flicking various knobs and switches – completely oblivious to the fact that his words had just left Ivy feeling like she'd been punched in the chest.

So - Gareth had decided that she didn't deserve the gorgeous cottage. Then he'd charged the motel to *her* credit card. He'd suggested they get a dog instead of proposing to her... and to top it all off, he'd stooped low enough to give her a Christmas present that was a bloody freebie he'd scrounged from work?!

'I'm Jock, by the way,' said the pilot, interrupting the tornado of righteous indignation that was building inside her. 'You all strapped in? Ready to go?'

Ivy nodded tightly. Yes – she was ready. She needed to get as far away from Gareth as was humanly possible. It might only be for an hour or so – but that hour was crucial right now.

'Excellent! Let's get this bird in the air!' said Jock, shooting her a wink.

As they started to trundle down the runway, Ivy wondered whether they'd be flying directly over the motel. She hoped so - she'd love nothing more than to be able to look down on Gareth and raise a festive middle finger in his direction.

Bollocking baubles to you, knobhead!

He could eat his breakfast in peace in the ghastly motel cafeteria while she took a private flight to a little island. What a way to spend Christmas Eve – she'd enjoy it just to spite him!

Ivy glanced around her. She'd never had an entire plane to herself – a private flight! How fancy?! Well... not in the usual way... but she could dream! No matter how determined she was to make the best out of the situation, she couldn't compare this old plane to a private jet... it wasn't exactly new *or* luxurious. It seemed to be held together with bits of chewing gum and chocolate wrappers that had been jammed down between the dozen or so seats.

Ivy wriggled, trying to get comfortable. There wasn't much legroom... and certainly no sign of an inflight magazine... or loo. Then again, it was such a short flight she guessed you really should be able to hold on for that long – even if you'd had a pint or two the night before!

Ivy turned to look behind her. Blimey – it really was tiny in here! Suddenly she realised that the seat diagonally behind her *did* have a passenger. It was a large net of brussel sprouts that had been carefully strapped in. She raised her eyebrows in bemusement. It had a label on the side. The words *Brussel Sprouts* had been crossed out and the word *Carrots!* Had been added in large, black letters instead. Only – these clearly weren't carrots - they were definitely brussel sprouts!

Weird!

Ivy leaned a little closer. She didn't want the pilot to think she was being nosy – but she *had* to check! Yep –

she wasn't seeing things – the net was crammed with the love-them-or-loathe-them mini brassicas of doom.

Shaking her head, turned back to the window as the plane gave a lurch. They were climbing quickly, and Ivy suddenly realised that they had already cleared the airfield. Damnit - she'd missed her chance to swear at Gareth from a great height! Maybe it was a blessing in disguise though. It was time to just sit back and enjoy this bizarre experience for what it was – a short break she could use to calm down and get control of herself again. After all, she'd be heading back before she knew it… then all she had to look forward to was another awkward night.

Ivy gave a determined little nod. She'd escape reality for a little while and leave it until the return journey to face the fact that she wasn't going to get the festive fairy tale she'd been dreaming about. With a long sigh, Ivy watched the mainland coast disappear behind them as they headed out to sea.

CHAPTER 4

'And just ahead in the distance, you'll see Crumcarey.'

The pilot's voice startled Ivy as it crackled over the tinny speakers. The Scottish mainland hadn't even disappeared behind them, but Jock was right - she could already see the silhouette of Crumcarey looming against the horizon.

'You'll notice the other two islands that make up the archipelago...'

Ivy smiled to herself as she craned her neck to keep them in view. As Jock started reeling off facts and figures about the little trio of islands, she couldn't help but notice that he sounded... well... a bit bored. It was clear the poor guy had done this many, *many* times and knew the well-worn script inside out.

Even though the sight of their destination didn't seem to hold any excitement for her pilot, Ivy felt a strange tingle travel down her spine. Crumcarey nestled under its own bank of cloud, looking strangely contented considering it looked like it was about to get some serious rain... or snow... or hail... She wasn't exactly sure which, but it was definitely about to welcome some serious weather!

'Crumcarey has two lochs,' Jock continued, his voice now settled into a monotonous drone that made Ivy want to giggle. 'Creatively enough, they're called Crum and Carey.'

Ivy tuned out the pilot's voice as she kept her eyes glued on the islands. She'd already read all about Crumcarey. The minute Gareth had mentioned this trip, she'd hopped online to do her research and found a blog post all about the place from someone who'd visited a couple of years ago. Crumcarey was the main island. Then, just off the south coast was a smaller land mass called Little Crum.

'The third and smallest island is called The Dot,' said the pilot with a long-suffering sigh. 'It sits at the north end of the main island and is only accessible during low tide via a causeway.'

According to the travel blogger Ivy had found, one of the locals claimed that The Dot was called The Dot because it was so small. It looked like someone had just dropped a biro on a map and left a mark - so a longer name would have been a bit silly. There had been a footnote stating that the blogger wasn't sure how accurate this particular piece of information might be, considering his source kept muttering things about sharks while he was being interviewed.

'If I can ask you to prepare for landing,' said Jock, his voice brightening up considerably.

Already?!

Ivy glanced around. It wasn't like she needed to do anything to prepare. They'd been in the air for such a short amount of time she hadn't even had the chance to remove her belt.

'Things may get a bit bumpy, I'm afraid,' said the Jock, sounding a lot more enthusiastic now. 'It's a bit blustery out there.'

Ivy swallowed down a nervous gulp of air. No matter how miffed she was with Gareth, right now she could do with him sitting next to her so that she could grab his hand and squeeze it until his fingers went blue. She took in a deep breath and let it out slowly... it'd be fine! She'd be fine. She didn't need him, did she?!

Because the plane was so small, Ivy could see right over Jock's shoulder from her seat. She stared out through the cockpit window as the plane lurched up and down, bouncing several feet at a time. She did her best to bite back a squeal of fright. There wasn't any sign of the islands ahead of them... let alone a runway... but they were losing height fast.

Whipping around to look out of her own window, she was horrified to find the strip of tarmac far to their right-hand side... and they appeared to be being blown sideways towards it.

'Isn't... isn't that the runway over there?' she said, her voice high and quavering.

'Please don't talk to the pilot while he's trying to fly the plane,' muttered Jock.

The fact that he was suddenly referring to himself in third person did nothing to calm Ivy's nerves. The words *"trying* to fly the plane" were just the icing on the cake. She quickly crossed her fingers on both hands, holding them stiffly in her lap as she tried to ignore the way the plane was now thumping up and down.

The wings seemed to be juddering. This couldn't be good, could it? Sure, she didn't much fancy being back with grumpy Gareth in the motel, but frankly, she'd give anything to be off this plane right now. Two minutes ago, it had felt like she was being whisked away for a magical, festive moment she'd never forget. Now it felt more like she was on a fair ride straight out of a horror novel.

Forcing herself not to close her eyes, Ivy turned to stare fixedly at the back of Jock's head as the plane did another doom-filled judder. Just as she was about to start really panicking, she felt her whole body swerve with the plane, and the runway arced into view at the front.

Jock pulled back on what Ivy could only imagine was the plane's version of a steering wheel, and they dropped quickly. Then, with barely a whisper of a thump, the plane settled onto the tarmac.

'Wow!' the gasp left Ivy in a rush of admiration and relief.

'Sorry, sorry!' said Jock. 'It's usually a bit smoother than that!'

Ivy didn't say anything – she was too full of admiration that they hadn't been blown off course to Scandinavia instead. Considering it was blowing an absolute hoolie outside – enough that the plane seemed to be rocking on its landing gear with each gust - she was just glad to be out of the air in one piece.

Leaning back, Ivy willed her heart rate to return to something a bit less frantic as they careered down the short runway. They came to a trundling halt next to a building that looked very much like a garden shed with a conservatory attached.

Ivy stared at it. *This* was the airport?! From what she could see through her little window, the whole thing looked like it was tethered to the ground. Wire guy ropes stretched between the building and several giant lumps of concrete that were bolted to the tarmac for good measure.

A wooden sign swinging dangerously from the front of the shed read *Crumcarey Island Airport.* There was a smaller sign hanging from hooks below it that read *Arrivals*. The moment they came to a standstill, someone scuttled out from the shed, bent double against the wind. Ivy watched as they unhooked the smaller sign with some difficulty, flipped it over and then hung it back up so that it now read *Departures*.

Their job done, the figure hurried straight back inside again.

'Well, here we are then!' said Jock as the engines powered down.

Ivy smiled. She was still staring out of the window, and her eyes had just wandered past the airport towards a tantalizing glimpse of the sea beyond. Then her smile promptly dropped. Out of nowhere, it started raining. Sideways. Huge drops whipped along the length of the plane, drawing splattered, soggy lines across her view.

'Right, let's be having you!' said Jock cheerfully, as he prized himself out of his chair and moved to open the door.

'Eh?' said Ivy, turning to him in a bit of a daze.

He made ushering motions at her as if he was trying to sweep her towards the steps that had just appeared outside as if by magic.

'Can't I just stay here until we're ready to go back?' she said, eyeballing the driving rain with a little shiver. After all – this trip had always been about the plane ride. She'd done that now, and they'd be heading off again in a matter of... half an hour or so? Sure, if the sun had been out, she'd have loved to have a quick look around. But now the weather was doing its thing quite so thoroughly out there, she'd much prefer to stay where she was.

'Nope!' said Jock firmly. 'You need to disembark. I need to refuel, and no one's allowed on board until that's done and I've had the chance to do my list of preflight checks!'

Ivy heaved herself to her feet and grabbed her handbag as Jock urged her forwards towards the steps.

'Make sure you hold on to the railing on the way down!' said Jock as Ivy paused at the top of the steps, screwing up her face as well as her courage before stepping out into the elements.

'Wow!' she gasped.

The minute she stepped out from the shelter of the plane, a gust of wind hit her like a speeding sleigh. She hastily wrapped her hands around the railings on either side of the set of steps. She'd love nothing more than to pause to button up her coat and pull up her hood – but there was no way she was letting go again until she was safely on the ground. Besides, she was already soaked to the skin!

'We'll be off in about thirty minutes!' yelled Jock the moment she reached the relative safety of the tarmac. 'So don't go too far!'

Ivy turned to ask him where she should go in the meantime – only for the rain to ramp up another notch and splatter her in the face. It felt a bit like being in one of those multi-directional showers you got in posh hotels – only the water in those didn't tend to be quite so icy! Unfortunately, Jock had already disappeared back inside the plane... and there was no way she'd risk those steps again – not in this wind.

Ivy stared around, feeling lost and more than a little

bit miffed. She couldn't exactly just stand around here on the tarmac like a very soggy lemon for half an hour, could she? Perhaps she should head over and see if they'd be willing for her to shelter inside the airport-shed-conservatory combo?! It might not be far – but the rain was now sheeting across the runway hard enough that she could barely see it in front of her.

Just as she was about to make a mad dash for it, a figure appeared from nowhere, making straight for the plane. They rushed past her and jogged easily up the steps. Two seconds later, they reappeared carrying the bag of "carrots".

Ivy watched in complete confusion as this woman – she could now see her face - made her way carefully back down the steps and then half-walked, half-jogged off into the rain. Maybe she should follow? After all… those "carrots" had to be heading somewhere warm and dry, didn't they?

Just at that moment, Jock reappeared at the top of the steps and stared at her in surprise.

'Why… rain… still here?'

Ivy could see that he was shouting down to her, but she could only catch a word here and there - the rest were whipped away by the wind. She shrugged helplessly, blinking as the rain continued to splatter into her face.

Jock pointed to her and then twice - rather forcefully - at the retreating back of the woman bearing the "carrots".

'…go…Tallyaff… depart… I'll find you!"

Right – that settled it. She had no idea what the word *Tallyaff* meant, but it was clear that the pilot wanted her to follow the woman. Not ideal – but the rain was starting to soak through her wildly inappropriate red wool coat, and her legs were aching from battling the violent gusts of wind.

It didn't really matter to Ivy where she went at this point, so long as it gave her somewhere warm and dry to shelter for a few minutes. Jock knew where she was going even if she didn't – so she'd just have to trust that he would come and find her when it was time to leave.

'Go… quick!'

This time she definitely caught the pilot's impatient order and Ivy hurried off after the slightly bent figure of the woman who'd almost disappeared behind curtains of pelting rain.

With any luck, wherever she was going would have a plastic cup of instant coffee with Ivy's name on it… and perhaps even a stale sandwich or biscuit or something. It wasn't as though she could expect much in a place as remote as this, but frankly, as long as it gave her something to warm her hands up on, that's all she really cared about right now.

Buoyed by the thought of a hot drink, Ivy picked up her pace and broke into a soggy jog, determined not to lose sight of her guide.

CHAPTER 5

❄

*L*uckily, there didn't seem to be any kind of security or fences to get through to leave the airport – so Ivy just put her head down and dashed through the pelting rain after the woman lugging the net of sprouts pretending to be carrots. Unfortunately, it didn't take long before she managed to lose sight of her.

Ivy was just about to start panicking when a building materialised right in front of her. Despite the torrential downpour, she came to an abrupt standstill. Doing her best to blink raindrops away from her eyelashes, she stared at the place. It didn't look particularly inviting – but then that was becoming something of a recurring theme on this trip – what with the motel and its sticky carpets. Still – this time she was just after a sanctuary from the weather for a few minutes, so it didn't really matter.

Ivy squinted at the sign on the front and mouthed the name, trying to wrap her lips around the unfamiliar word.

Tallyaff.

It was a two-storey stone building with small windows and what looked like very thick walls. It was foreboding... and a bit dour... and she didn't hold out much hope of a warm welcome. Frankly, the place could resemble the worst kind of public toilet and she'd be glad to get inside. The rain was making its way down her spine in an icy rivulet. It was time to get under shelter!

As though the weather was urging her to get on with things, an almighty gust of wind chose that moment to shove her in the back - practically blowing her through the door of the Tallyaff.

'Wow!' she squeaked in surprise, as she clung to the doorframe for support. Ivy couldn't help but wonder if a net of veggies was actually an essential item for anyone trying to stay on their feet on this windswept island – just for the added ballast!

Straightening up and closing the door firmly behind her, Ivy pushed her sodden hood off her equally drenched hair. It took her a moment to reorientate herself now that a howling gale wasn't blowing insistently in her earholes.

Well... this definitely wasn't what she'd been expecting. If Ivy was being honest, she'd been hoping for a kind of village hall vibe at best – complete with lino on the floor, ugly, orange plastic chairs stacked up in a corner and maybe a raised stage with some tatty velvet curtains to complete the effect. Either that or a hostel with a basic reception area and one of those instant hot-drinks machines which always had some kind of dodgy soup-in-a-cup option.

This was nothing like that. Not even slightly.

Ivy was in a little entrance vestibule – clearly designed to keep the cosiness in and the weather firmly out. It was a clean, flag-stoned space with various pairs of boots lined up neatly against one wall, and an old-fashioned coat stand tucked into a corner. Through a glass-panelled double door, she could see a large room glinting at her, golden and inviting.

Hastily peeling off her coat, Ivy hung it up, making sure it wouldn't drip on anything important, and then toed her soggy trainers off too. She'd take her lead from all the other boots out here - it didn't seem polite to wander in and make their floors all wet!

Feeling slightly self-conscious about padding into this unknown place in her damp, socked feet, Ivy cracked open the door. A warm blast of fragrant air hit her in the face – the comforting scents of cinnamon, coffee and sweet baking almost bringing tears to her eyes. Any hesitation she had about being here disappeared instantly. She quickly slipped inside and closed the door behind her.

Ivy looked around, wondering what had become of

her guide. Despite the line-up of boots out in the entrance, it looked like she was the only one there.

A shiver took her by surprise. She hadn't realised how cold she'd managed to get on the short walk from the airport, but now that she was surrounded by glorious warmth, she was suddenly aware that her hands and feet felt like ice blocks. It shouldn't take her too long to defrost in here though.

Ivy moved forward, her feet padding silently over the aged-polished floorboards and onto a slightly motheaten rug that felt a bit like heaven under her chilly tootsies.

The room was large and rather beautiful – in a fire-lit, homely sort of way. Over to her right, there was an area that clearly doubled as a bit of a grocery store for the island. It was ridiculously well stocked. Even from where she was standing, Ivy could see that they had all three varieties of jam she liked - their distinctive lids were an instant giveaway. There was a good selection of bread and delicious-looking pastries that made her stomach growl, and a glass-fronted fridge full of milk and cheese.

On the opposite side of the space was a huge wood burner set in an ancient fireplace. The old thing was belting out heat – and Ivy could feel her entire body being drawn to the squashy-looking armchairs in front of it. But maybe she should at least let someone know she was here first!

It didn't look like there was any kind of reception

desk. Instead, directly in front of her, spanning the entire length of the far wall, was a bar. A couple of draft taps gleamed in the golden light, and a ridiculously long line of optics sat proudly on the wall behind the bar. It looked like this place wore many hats – shop, sitting room, bar and... guesthouse? It was certainly *much* nicer than the motel!

There still wasn't any sign of human life though, and Ivy really didn't feel comfortable being here without checking it was okay with someone first! Besides, those pastries in the little grocery section had set her stomach grumbling... but she couldn't just help herself, could she?!

'Hello?' she called, wincing slightly as her voice echoed around the space.

'Hello!'

Ivy jumped as a woman appeared as if by magic behind the bar.

'Sorry – didn't mean to startle you!' laughed the stranger, slinging a tea towel over her shoulder. 'I was just popping some mince pies in the oven. I didn't realise you were here!'

Ivy smiled at her. It was impossible not to – the mellow Scottish accent warmed something in her heart just as much as the wood burner was working its magic on the rest of her. This had to be the woman she'd just chased back from the airport.

'Just off the plane?' she asked, tilting her head, her eyes darting to the door and then back to Ivy.

Ivy nodded, trying to ignore another loud growl from her stomach. She wrapped her arms around herself in the hope it might muffle the sound a bit. The woman's appearance had brought a delicious waft of fresh baking from what Ivy assumed was the kitchen. She couldn't quite place what the smell was – but it was definitely something Christmassy. Sweet and spicy and mouth-wateringly yummy. Maybe a cake or pudding... or warm, spiced wine?

'I'm Olive,' said the woman. 'Olive Martinelli. Can I get you anything? You look a bit... chilly...'

'I don't want to be a bother,' said Ivy quickly, for some reason feeling ridiculously *English.*

'Bother?' laughed Olive, 'It would be my pleasure. How about a coffee... or maybe a mulled wine to warm you up properly?'

'A coffee would be lovely, please,' said Ivy.

If she was being honest, a mulled wine sounded even better – but she wasn't sure how Gareth would react if she came back stinking of booze – even if it *was* Christmas Eve. Then again, did she really care what he thought? He was probably back in their horrible motel room coming up with a list of names for their hypothetical dog.

'Latte?' prompted Olive, catching Ivy just in time to stop her spirits from disappearing down a Gareth-related black hole. 'Cappuccino? Espresso? Macchiato? Americano? Flat white?'

Ivy laughed in surprise. She hadn't been expecting

that! Her head was still stuck in her preconceived notion that the best she could hope for was an instant made from coffee granules that had to be mined from the sticky mass left over at the bottom of a jar!

'Latte please,' she said.

'Any syrup with that?' said Olive. 'We're out of caramel until the New Year, but I've got vanilla, gingerbread or hazelnut.

'Oooh – gingerbread please!' said Ivy. The idea of a silky-smooth Christmassy latte that she could sip in front of the roaring wood burner made her wriggle with delight.

'Anything to eat?' said Olive. 'There's a whole load of chocolate croissants warming in the oven. We were expecting a few more people on that flight if I'm honest.'

Ivy noticed Olive's eyes flit to the door again. She was clearly expecting a bunch of rowdy lads to appear at any moment.

'Apparently, it was a stag do,' said Ivy. 'According to the pilot, they were "unavoidably delayed."'

'Happens quite a lot!' snorted Olive. 'It all seems like fun and games - booking everyone in for the flight over here - until it comes to the morning. Then they're more worried about keeping their breakfast down – that's if they can manage any in the first place!' Olive paused and rolled her eyes. 'So... can I tempt you with a pastry?'

'I'd *love* one!' said Ivy, beaming back at her. It was

impossible not to with the wave of warmth that was pouring off this woman. Ivy could feel the nervous tension leaving her shoulders and she let out a sigh as her whole body started to relax. 'You know – this place is amazing?! I don't know what I was expecting after being the only passenger on that tiny plane sitting next to a bag of brussel sprouts – but it wasn't this!'

'Carrots,' said the woman.

'Erm... sorry?' laughed Ivy.

'The bag on the plane. It was carrots. You must have been mistaken.'

Ivy laughed again, but then stopped abruptly when she realised that the smiley woman was suddenly looking very serious.

'Erm... they were definitely sprouts?' she said, the inflection in her voice making her sound anything but definite. What was this, some kind of weird, vegetable-based gaslighting?!

Olive looked over her shoulder, clearly checking that there were definitely alone.

'Weird bylaw of Crumcarey Island,' she whispered, leaning conspiratorially across the bar and beckoning Ivy in closer. 'Sprouts have been banned on the island since 1953. The ban's in place all year, but it's even more strict at Christmas.'

'You're kidding?!' said Ivy, her lips twitching. She was desperate to laugh.

'Nope, dead serious,' said Olive, shaking her head, her eyes twinkling. 'So, you see... it would be illegal to import a bag of sprouts for the wonderful Christmas dinner I'm going to be preparing for everyone tomorrow.'

'Oh,' said Ivy, still wondering if this was all a big joke. Maybe Gareth had cooked it up. Maybe she should be checking for hidden cameras right about now... what if it was all some kind of weird, extended way to propose to her off-guard?

Nah – if one thing this fiasco of a trip had taught her so far, it was that Gareth simply didn't have it in him.

'So,' continued Olive, 'as the chair of the Chamber of Commerce, secretary of the Tourist Board, governor of the ferry company and proprietor of this guest-house... I *would* never and *could* never be seen doing such a thing as smuggling sprouts onto the island for Christmas dinner. Instead... we have to make do with carrots!'

'Right!' said Ivy, finally cottoning on. 'Carrots!'

'Carrots!' said Olive again, grinning at her and then giving her a firm wink and straightening up. 'Now then – I'll bring that coffee and croissant over – you look like you need warming up. Head over there and take a seat by the fire – I'll be right back!'

CHAPTER 6

❄

Ivy slumped down onto one of the squishy tartan armchairs next to the raging wood burner and stared moodily out of the window at the driving rain. The heavy drops were beating against the glass as if they were trying to force their way inside.

So much for getting a chance to look around outside while she was here - that walk from the airport had been more than enough weather for Ivy for one day! Any thought of taking a quick peek at the scenery, enjoying a stroll on one of the beaches and maybe grabbing a couple of photos promptly vanished. She turned away from the rain-washed window and let the warmth of the fire begin to seep into her bones.

Scraping her hair to one side, Ivy surreptitiously squeezed a stream of raindrops onto the flagstones. Oops! Still, better than soaking the back of this gorgeous armchair! It was super-soft and comfortable - in the way only an old and much-loved armchair could be. Ivy snuggled back into its depths, glad to have the chance to warm up properly – especially as there was coffee and a pastry on the way. As long as she had enough time to enjoy them before she had to get back on the plane, all would be well with the world... or at least it *would* be until they touched down on the mainland again.

Ivy gave a little shudder as she thought about the motel. Maybe she could convince Gareth to up-sticks and find that cosy cottage after all. She was sure she could plead with the owners to let them have a last-minute booking - that's if it was still available. It did seem a bit unlikely considering it was Christmas Eve. Still, it would be worth a try.

Maybe enjoying a couple of nights of cosy luxury together would help fix this whole fiasco and get them back on track. Ivy shook her head and let out a long sigh. She was starting to wonder if it wasn't just a case of their relationship being a bit de-railed – somehow it felt more like the tracks had been dynamited.

It hadn't always been like this between her and Gareth. They'd had a lot of fun at the start... and he'd been sweet... in his way. Now she knew him well enough to be familiar with all his little foibles. When Gareth decided he was right about something, he'd dig his heels in like the flipping festive ass he was!

Ah well, she needed to enjoy this brief respite before getting back to what might end up being the most miserable Christmas she'd ever had the misfortune to experience.

In a bid to distract herself from her doom-laden thoughts, Ivy stared at the collection of photographs displayed above the mantle of the old fireplace. The entire wall was covered in a motley collection – some in frames and some just tacked up with pins or tape.

There were fishermen and their boats. Pool tournament winners from 1976. Someone in a mini excavator drinking a glass of wine. This photo made Ivy smile – it was just so incongruous! Then there were various portraits of the different ferry boats through the ages – the first one looked like it had sails!

The photos weren't hung in any order and not a single one of them was straight... but the overall effect was glorious. This was a wall full of community history and spirit. It made Ivy's heartache and long for something... but she couldn't quite put her finger on what it was!

'Here we go!'

Olive's voice cut across Ivy's sudden bout of wistful heartache, and she twisted in her seat only to come face to face with a fragrant tray of deliciousness. Before she knew what was happening, there was a pretty plate sitting on the low table in front of her, complete with chocolate croissant and linen napkin.

Olive quickly added a piping-hot mug of coffee. The scent of the warm, gingerbread syrup curled up from the coffee cup and wound its way around Ivy. Suddenly she felt like curling up in her chair and staying put until New Year.

'Now then. I wasn't sure what kind of pastry eater you were,' said Olive, laying a knife and fork next to her plate. 'Knife, fork or fingers? Either way, it's always a pain for you to have to ask so I thought I'd hedge my bets! Just… tell me you're not a spoon person!'

Ivy grinned at her and shook her head. 'Definitely not a spoon person,' she said, picking up the pastry and tearing it in half with her fingers.

'Girl after my own heart,' said Olive approvingly, her eyes on the flurry of pastry flakes that had just landed on Ivy's jumper. 'I can see that you and I are going to get along famously! Try it!' she insisted.

Ivy didn't need to be told twice. She tore off a chunk and popped it in her mouth, closing her eyes as the warm, buttery, chocolatey goodness made her cheeks ache.

'Do you like it?' asked Olive, a knowing grin on her face.

Ivy opened her eyes and nodded enthusiastically – not daring to say anything as she didn't want to spray this angel of mercy with bits of pastry.

'Is the coffee okay?' prompted Olive.

Ivy dutifully swallowed and took a sip of her drink.

She let out a groan of delight. Sure – she was cold and in desperate need of caffeine, but still - she was pretty certain she'd never tasted a cup of coffee quite this delicious in her entire life. It was rich and creamy and tasted of Christmas.

'Good, huh?!' laughed Olive in amusement. 'It's all down to the milk, you know - it's local. Mr Harris has a few cows over by Big Sandy. He's got a poorly ankle at the moment so we have to go and pick it up ourselves... but by the sound you're making, I reckon it's worth it?'

Ivy nodded again. 'Erm... Big Sandy?' she asked curiously.

'It's the beach over on the west side of the island,' said Olive, pottering over to the wood burner and bending low to throw another log into its depths. 'You've probably seen a photo of it if you looked us up on the internet – great big white sandy beach? It tends to be the main photo people like to use!'

'Ooh,' said Ivy, 'yep – I've seen it!' It had been the lead image on the travel blog. 'And there's a smaller one too, isn't there... called something similar?'

'Little Sandy over on the east coast,' said Olive. 'And then there's a beach down by the ferry port called Not Sandy... for obvious reasons.'

'Erm...?' said Ivy.

'It's pebbly!' laughed Olive. 'Not Sandy - get it?!'

Ivy grinned and nodded. She'd pored over every

photograph she'd been able to find when Gareth had first mentioned the flights to Crumcarey. Of course, back then, she'd been dreaming of finding the perfect backdrop for their loved-up, "newly engaged" photos. She'd spent a good half an hour imagining them both looking windswept and slightly bohemian on Big Sandy, with the massive, sparkling ring he'd given her as the centrepiece. The grin promptly slipped from Ivy's face.

Fat chance of that!

Never mind, she wasn't going to let thoughts of Gareth - sitting in the motel brooding over dog names - detract from this unexpectedly lovely break from reality. Ivy had to admit she was secretly happy that he hadn't come with her... and not just because it was giving her the chance to cool off a bit.

Gareth had always had the knack of being a killjoy when they went out together. He didn't really have an adventurous bone in his body. He'd have probably insisted on waiting at the airport, and even if by some miracle they had ended up here at the Tallyaff, he'd have gone into snob-overdrive. She'd seen him do it plenty of times before in cafes and restaurants – asking for something that wasn't available just to be annoying.

Even a coffee order was never a simple thing with Gareth around... he'd demand organic, or oat milk, or - knowing him - virgin alpaca milk. Not that there was anything wrong with any of those choices if that's what you *really* wanted – but Gareth didn't... he just did it to be as difficult as possible.

Ivy frowned as she took another sip of creamy coffee. *Why* was she having such a hard time getting her mind off Gareth's bad points? Poor guy – she wasn't really being fair. She was sure she wasn't all sweetness and light to deal with herself!

'It's organic too, you know,' said Olive, who was still hovering.

'Sorry?' said Ivy, realising she'd been miles away.

'The milk!' chuckled Olive. 'It's organic.'

'Oh!' said Ivy, with a polite smile. Blimey – was this woman some kind of mind reader?

'I should have mentioned it before,' said Olive, 'but it never seems like that big a deal here – and I forget visitors like to know. We don't use any pesticides or artificial nasties on the island. Not that there would be much point in bug sprays, if I'm honest - they get blown off into the North Atlantic before they can do much damage! And we use seaweed for fertiliser. That's what our farmers have been using for hundreds of years... can't see them stopping now!'

'Oh,' said Ivy. She wasn't quite sure what to say. 'Erm... that's probably quite a selling point for your tourist board?'

'Yes... it could be,' said Olive. 'I mean – we're not certified or anything. For one thing, it'd be quite hard to get an inspector to come all the way out here. Besides that, Mr Harris has got a dog – and McGregor doesn't take kindly to strangers, so Mr Harris has never bothered.'

'Still,' said Ivy, 'it could get you some great publicity!'

'Now, don't get me wrong,' said Olive with a shrug, 'we *do* love the visitors we get, but we don't want to be overrun. I think the whole "hidden gem" thing we've got going on is all we need. Crumcarey pops up now and then in one of those "ten undiscovered destinations" articles – and that's more than enough to keep a steady trickle of visitors coming in!'

'But imagine "Crumcarey Organic Dairy" though!' said Ivy.

'Mr Harris already sells out… so there's not much point!' laughed Olive. 'We buy most of his milk for the Tallyaff and the shop… and now the rest of it goes to the ice cream van!'

'There's an ice cream van?' said Ivy. Somehow she couldn't imagine one of those up here… not with the rain still trying to batter its way through the windows!

Olive nodded, her eyes twinkling. 'My daughter moved back up here at the end of the summer and brought Ruby – her van – home with her. And Frank too, of course. That's her new man. Lovely lad he is too!'

Ivy smiled politely. 'And they're selling ice creams?'

'Oh yes!' said Olive. 'They seem to do alright when it's raining for some reason… which is good because it rains a lot. But I'm guessing the customers will dry up when there's a foot of fresh snow on the ground.'

'But they're staying on Crumcarey all winter?' said Ivy.

'Now that Stella's met Frank, I'll bet you anything the pair of them will be on the island for the rest of their lives,' said Olive. 'You should see them – happy as larks together. Makes my heart glad, I can tell you, to see my little girl find her other half.'

Ivy nodded stiffly, her heart hammering uncomfortably against the sudden lump in her throat. *That* was what love should feel like... pure bliss wherever you were. Not misunderstandings and petty squabbles and five-am-rants about dog walking schedules.

'I'm sorry my dear,' said Olive, clearly unaware of Ivy's discomfort. 'Listen to me going on! I'll leave you to enjoy your coffee in peace before Jock arrives to collect you for your flight home.'

Ivy started to shake her head, not wanting Olive to think she was rude, but the older woman smiled. 'I've got a mountain of *carrots* that won't prepare themselves!'

With that, Olive winked at Ivy and strode off towards the kitchen.

❄

Ten minutes later, Ivy heaved herself reluctantly to her feet and brushed pastry crumbs from her jumper. No matter how hard she'd tried to get back into the cosy spirit of this little adventure she was meant to be enjoying, a heavy weight had settled on her heart. It wasn't that she was jealous of Olive's daughter for finding her perfect match… it was more a feeling of total fear that she'd been about to agree to marry Gareth… if he'd asked.

Was he her other half?

Right now, he simply wasn't fitting Olive's perfect portrait of how that should feel.

Ivy didn't really want to go back to the airport, but there wasn't much choice in the matter was there? It was time to get back to reality. Picking up her empty cup and plate, Ivy took them over to the bar.

As if by magic, Olive appeared.

'Everything okay for you?' she asked, her eyes sweeping the empty plate and cup with an approving smile.

'Gorgeous, thanks!' said Ivy, fiddling around with her handbag as she tried to get her purse out from its depths. 'How much do I owe you?'

'Hold that thought,' said Olive as her eyes darted over Ivy's shoulder towards the door.

Ivy turned, only to see Jock the pilot beckoning for Olive to join him.

'Excuse me a moment,' said Olive, throwing her tea towel down on the bar.

Ivy raised her eyebrows as she watched Olive hurry over towards him. She was no student of body language, but from the way the pair of them huddled together, shooting the occasional worried look in her direction, it was pretty obvious there was something going on. Something... very wrong.

There was a swift, muttered conversation between the pair of them. Ivy strained her ears but failed to catch a single word. Then Jock started making strange, sharp movements with his hands as if he was demonstrating how to snap an invisible twig.

Uh oh – that couldn't be good!

Olive nodded at Jock, making ushering motions as if she was trying to sweep him back outside, before turning back to Ivy with a very deliberate, over-bright smile.

'What's up?' said Ivy, as Olive headed back behind the bar.

'Would you like to take out a tab with us, deary?' asked Olive. 'I'm afraid it looks like you're not going to be able to leave for a little while yet.'

'Why?' said Ivy. 'What's wrong?

'Well,' she said, 'it looks like there's been some kind of malfunction on the plane. Jock's not quite sure what it is at the moment, but he should know a bit more in a few hours!'

'A few hours?!' groaned Ivy.

'Ah well,' said Olive, cheerfully. 'At least you're safe and sound on the ground – so that's something to be grateful for, isn't it? And you're welcome to wait here in the warm.'

'But… I *do* really need to get back,' said Ivy faintly. 'I mean… it's Christmas Eve.'

'I know, dearie,' said Olive sympathetically. 'But let's put it like this - that plane won't be going anywhere for a good while and neither will you. I'm afraid you're stuck on Crumcarey for the time being!'

CHAPTER 7

❄

No need to panic. There's no need to panic!
But it was almost Christmas, for goodness' sake – this wasn't the plan!

Ivy took a deep breath. She needed to calm down. She was sure the plane would be fixed in a jiffy. After all, it had been in the air with her on board not more than an hour ago, so it couldn't be anything too serious, could it?! Jock would get it fixed and she'd be on her way back to the mainland before she knew it... back to spend Christmas day with her wonderful fiancé, Gareth.

Suddenly, Ivy slumped. She had to face facts - the broken plane wasn't her only problem. It wasn't even the most *serious* problem, was it?!

Gareth wasn't her fiancé - because he hadn't proposed. In fact, it was now pretty clear that he'd never intended to propose – at least, not marriage!

Asking her to get a big, hairy dog wasn't *quite* the same thing.

It was official. So far, this Christmas sucked. It wasn't going the way she'd hoped and planned for... and there was nothing Ivy hated more than when things didn't go according to plan.

'Are you alright?' asked Olive, looking at her with concern.

'I'm fine,' said Ivy. 'Just fine... everything's... fine.' She stopped herself, willing her bottom lip to stop wobbling. Who was she trying to convince here – Olive or herself?! 'It's just that it's Christmas... and it's gone wrong. About as wrong as it can go... and it was supposed to be perfect.'

'I'm sure it's not all that bad,' said Olive, kindly. 'Why don't you have another coffee to cheer you up a bit? And I've got some newly baked mince pies just out of the oven... or there's a custard tart... or another pastry?'

Ivy bit her lip. She would not cry... she *would* not cry!

'A coffee sounds perfect,' she said at last, her voice high and tight. With any luck, the extra jolt of caffeine might just stop her from blubbing. Maybe. She was tempted to have another croissant too – the first one had been mouth-wateringly gorgeous after all - but she decided against it.

'Are you sure I can't get you something to eat?' said Olive. 'I've got plenty. If you can't decide between them, you could always have a mince pie *and* a custard tart! It *is* nearly Christmas, you know!'

As if to prove her point, Olive reached sideways and hit the switch on a stuffed, smiling Christmas tree that sat on the bar in front of the beer taps. The moment she touched it, the thing sprang to life and started singing Jingle Bells. Its dance moves, however, were far from family-friendly – in fact, the little thing looked like it was taking inspiration straight from Magic Mike.

A giggle burst out of Ivy in a kind of explosion, making both her and Olive jump. She promptly clapped her hand over her mouth, her eyes wide with a combination of mirth and horror.

'That's more like it!' said Olive, grinning at her, and giving the grinding Christmas tree an approving pat, setting it off again. 'Now then… a little plate of goodies to see you through your wait?'

Ivy relented with a grateful nod. 'Yes, please!'

Deciding against returning to her original chair next to the wood burner, Ivy slipped onto one of the stools next to the bar instead. It didn't seem fair to make Olive run around all over the place after her – especially as she wasn't even meant to be here. Besides, it would be nice to have someone to chat to for a bit.

Two seconds later, Olive returned and placed a plate bearing not one, but three sweet treats in front of Ivy. She stared down at the delicious trio of mince pie, custard tart and chocolate pastry - and felt her mouth water.

'You'll be needing this, I expect!' said Olive, handing over a fresh linen napkin with a grin.

'Thank you,' said Ivy, grabbing it and then eyeballing the plate as she tried to decide where to start.

In a matter of moments, Olive placed a steaming mug of fresh coffee next to her, adding a hefty dollop of syrup to it for good measure.

At last, Ivy made a decision and bit into the mince pie. She had to force herself not to let out an indecent groan as the pastry melted and her mouth was flooded with the taste of Christmas.

'Mmmmm!' she said.

Well… she'd *tried* to keep it in!

'Glad you approve!' chuckled Olive.

'Officially the best mince pie I've ever tasted!' she said, licking crumbs from her lips.

'I might quote you on that for the website!' said Olive, with a broad smile.

'Fine by me!' said Ivy. She took a sip of coffee and let out a little sigh. There were definitely worse places to be stuck waiting for a flight on Christmas Eve!

Doing her best to pace herself, Ivy turned to look around again, taking in the handful of Christmas decorations that added a few red, gold and green touches here and there. That's when the decided lack of a Christmas tree hit her. It didn't seem quite right, somehow – and there was certainly plenty of space for one.

'Can I ask…' Ivy turned back to Olive, but then hesitated. The last thing she wanted to do was offend Olive – especially after the woman had been so kind to her.

'Ask away, dear!' said Olive, polishing a pint glass with a fresh tea towel before reaching up to stash it on a high shelf behind the bar.

'I was just wondering why you'd decided against a Christmas tree,' said Ivy, sounding slightly sheepish.

'It's funny how visitors always notice the lack of tree,' laughed Olive, starting to polish another glass. 'We get the same question every year!'

'Oh sorry,' said Ivy quickly. 'I didn't mean to be rude!'

'It's not rude at all,' said Olive. 'Just funny – it really does happen every year. That's how we ended up with Cliff here.'

'Cliff?' said Ivy in confusion.

'Yes – this is Cliff,' said Olive, patting the stuffed, dancing Christmas tree and setting him off again, making Ivy grin. 'One of our regular visitors took pity on our lack of tree a couple of years ago and sent him to us as a present.'

'Nice!' laughed Ivy.

'Not quite the same, I know,' said Olive, smiling at Cliff the Christmas tree fondly. 'But you see, there aren't really any trees on the island, so if we wanted a Christmas tree, it'd have to come over by ferry.'

'And that's not possible?' said Ivy in surprise.

'Oh yes, it's possible!' said Olive. 'I know for a fact it wouldn't be a problem for Connor to get his hands on one. He usually gets one for himself and anyone else who wants one. He captains the ferry you see, and lugs all sorts of things over from the mainland – whatever the community needs. But Christmas trees in the Tallyaff tend to cause arguments for some reason. I don't know what it is about them, but I've decided that they're simply not worth the aggravation.'

'What kind of arguments?' asked Ivy, her voice coming out muffled from behind a mouthful of custard tart.

'Oh - you know - the usual,' said Olive, focusing on yet another pint glass. 'It should have been a spruce rather than a pine. It should have been Norwegian instead of a Noble. It should smell... it *shouldn't* smell. It should have been decorated in gold, not silver. It should be traditional, not modern. It's just not worth it!'

Ivy nodded along as she sipped her coffee. It was just as good as the first one had been – though she could now feel the magical caffeine sloshing through her veins, making her heart pound. She'd be bouncing off the ceiling if she had too many more of these!

'I happen to be the Executive Officer for the Decorations and Festivities Committee,' said Olive, drawing herself up importantly before shooting Ivy a quick wink. 'The Tallyaff is basically the community living room – so every year we have to hold a vote on whether to get a tree. Every year there's an argument about it, and we decide not to bother - even though I've got all the tinsel and baubles in the box under the stairs. You might have noticed that I don't tend to decorate the place too heavily either – not until the last minute, anyway. Otherwise, people just think I'm trying to work my way up towards getting a tree by stealth. They're a suspicious lot around here.'

Ivy noticed that even though her words might sound a bit harsh, Olive had a huge, warm smile on her face. She clearly adored everything about her home here on Crumcarey.

'Sounds like a classic, family Christmas to me,' said Ivy with a smile. 'Christmas isn't Christmas without the traditional arguments!'

'Oh yes,' said Olive warmly, 'I couldn't agree more. We're such a small community, the whole island is like one big family. Of course, I'm lucky that my actual family is here too – I live over near Big Sandy with my husband, and I've already told you about Stella coming home!'

'I had a tree once.'

The voice right behind Ivy made her jump in fright, sending little bits of pastry skittering across the bar. She hadn't realised that there was a single soul in The Tallyaff besides her and Olive.

Willing her heart back into its usual spot, she turned to find a very old, very short man standing right next to her. He stared at her intently for a few seconds before turning his gaze to her rapidly emptying plate.

'I'll have one of your mince pies, Olive, if your friend hasn't eaten them all?'

Olive grinned and dashed off to the kitchen without saying anything. So – this was clearly a local, then!

'You don't mind if I sit, do you?' he said to Ivy. 'Bad ankle.'

Before Ivy could respond, the old man plonked himself down onto the bar stool next to her. Or at least, he did after several attempts to lift himself up high enough. He managed it in the end though and balanced his sticks against the wooden bar next to him with a grunt of relief.

'I won't tell you what colour it is today,' he said, 'because I can't. I haven't looked – turns my stomach a bit before breakfast, if I'm honest, so I slept in my socks. Then McGregor here wanted to go outside, so I didn't get the chance.'

'McGregor?' said Ivy, confused.

'Aye, lass. The dog,' he said.

'Oh,' said Ivy in surprise as she glanced down at the base of his stool only to lock eyes with a scruffy little wiry-haired dog. It had an even more intense stare than its master – or, it would have if it wasn't ever so slightly cross-eyed. Ivy thought that it looked more than a little bit grumpy – but maybe that was just the effect of the ragged fringe of fur half-covering its eyes.

'Hello, McGregor,' she said faintly.

The dog didn't take its eyes off her. It didn't even blink. Was this the dog Olive had mentioned earlier… the one who hated strangers? Maybe tickles were out of the question until she found out for sure!

'I'm Mr Harris,' said the newcomer, holding out his hand for her to shake. Ivy shook it on autopilot, then almost gasped in surprise. His skin was ridiculously soft.

'Thought old hands like mine would be as rough as sandpaper, didn't you lass?' he chuckled. He'd clearly been watching for her reaction. 'Not mine. I've milked cows all my life. Got to keep them nice and soft and supple. You get more milk that way. That's what I think, anyway.' He paused and gave her a toothy smile. Well, mostly toothy if you ignored the gummy gaps here and there.

Ivy didn't really know what to say. She couldn't exactly claim to know anything about whether soft hands meant more milk - she'd never really thought about it before.

'Now then,' said Mr Harris. 'I was telling you about my tree.'

'Tree?' said Ivy.

'Yes. Not a Christmas tree though. It was just a little twig of a thing. I'm not sure what kind it was, but it was right outside my kitchen window and it was getting quite tall, almost up to my knees, and then the cows ate it. Shame, I say. It was a crying shame.' He fell silent and gazed into the semi-distance.

Ivy bit her lip, trying not to giggle. Obviously, the story was over, but she didn't really have a clue what it had to do with Christmas trees. Thankfully, at that moment, Olive reappeared and placed a plate with a couple of warm mince pies in front of him.

'Coffee with that?' she asked. 'Usual? How's the ankle?'

'Aye, usual,' said Mr Harris – which was completely unnecessary as Olive had already turned to the gleaming coffee machine. 'I was just telling the lass here, I haven't looked yet because McGregor wanted a walk.'

As if on cue, McGregor got to his feet. He still hadn't taken his eyes off Ivy, and suddenly seemed to have decided it was time to get to know her better. Ivy put her mug down on the bar and watched him nervously.

'Now then, McGregor, play nice,' said Mr Harris, picking up a mince pie and taking a bite, completely unconcerned.

The little dog moved towards Ivy and began sniffing suspiciously at her trousers. Ivy kept her socked feet completely still. She didn't want to spook McGregor – nor did she want to give him an exciting target by accidentally wriggling her toes.

McGregor sniffed one foot and then the other.

Then he took two steps back, gave a little growl, and shook his head before moving forwards and starting the elaborate ritual all over again. This went on for several minutes, during which time Ivy barely dared to breathe. Then, clearly making up his strange little doggy mind about something, McGregor promptly threw himself down right on top of Ivy's socked feet.

'Well I never,' said Mr Harris in surprise. 'He's decided you're one of us!'

'You should feel honoured, Ivy!' said Olive, raising her eyebrows as she craned over the bar to take a peek.

Ivy wasn't so sure about that. The dog was decidedly damp and she could already feel it seeping from his springy fur through the wool of her socks.

'Have you put in an order for your Christmas dinner yet?' said Mr Harris.

'I won't be here, I'm afraid,' said Ivy, shaking her head. 'I'm heading back to the mainland as soon as they get the plane sorted.'

'Never mind that,' said Mr Harris. 'You should stay. You'll enjoy it. Lovely carrots!' he added, giving her a huge wink.

'No, really, I won't be here,' said Ivy firmly. 'I'll be back on the mainland with my fiancé for Christmas.'

Mr Harris raised one bushy eyebrow. 'But you're stuck here, aren't you?' he asked, his voice sounding gentler now.

'Only until the plane's fixed,' said Ivy, repeating herself.

'I'd get your order in now - before someone else takes your place,' said Mr Harris, following suit.

Ivy felt a shiver run down her spine. Somehow, this old man's insistence and absolute certainty that she'd be joining them for Christmas dinner was making her feel like there were forces at work beyond her control.

'Leave the girl be,' chuckled Olive. 'I'm sure Jock'll be back before she's even finished that coffee.'

CHAPTER 8

❄

McGregor wriggled around on Ivy's feet, making himself even more comfortable. Ivy held her breath as the little dog flopped on his side, ensuring that both her socks were sharing the same damp, doggy treatment. She didn't dare turn around when she heard the entrance door give a little creak behind her for fear of dislodging her living, breathing pair of smelly slippers.

'Hello lad!' said Mr Harris, turning to grin at whoever it was. 'Fancy a coffee?'

'Thanks, Mr Harris, but I can't,' came a deep, quiet voice. 'Is Olive out in the kitchen?'

'Aye lad,' said Mr Harris, turning back and taking a sip of his double espresso, his mouth puckering.

Jock the pilot appeared at the end of the bar, and Ivy did everything in her power to lock eyes with him. He *had* to know more about the state of the plane by now, and as much as she was enjoying this weird interlude at the Tallyaff, she was quite keen to see how much of her original Christmas plan she could salvage... and that could only happen back on the mainland.

Jock, however, had other ideas and disappeared into the kitchen without meeting her eye. Ivy knew she was probably being paranoid, but she'd put money on the fact that he'd been avoiding her gaze on purpose.

Straining her ears, Ivy did her best to decipher the mumbling conversation going on just the other side of the kitchen door, but McGregor chose that moment to start snoring.

A couple of minutes later, Jock reappeared. He scuttled out of the kitchen, taking off his clip-on tie as he went, and then promptly headed for the exit at a rate of knots.

Ivy stared in surprise at his retreating back, and then turned back towards the bar, only to find Olive smiling at her kindly.

'Now then, Ivy,' she said. 'I'm afraid the plane is broken.'

Ivy nodded. 'I know... but how long's it going to take to get it sorted? Jock didn't say...'

'I don't think you understand,' said Olive gently. 'It's not going anywhere today, by the look of things.'

'So how am I going to get back to the mainland?' said Ivy, wincing at the tone of desperation in her voice.

Olive glanced at Mr Harris with her eyebrows raised, and Ivy watched as the old man did his best to stifle a smile.

'Well, you can't really,' she said slowly. 'Unless you can swim?' she added.

'I...' Ivy promptly shut her mouth, realising just in time that Olive was only joking.

'Sharks,' said Mr Harris under his breath.

'There aren't any sharks,' laughed Olive as she reached out and patted Ivy's hand reassuringly. 'Or at least – none that can hurt you! Don't listen to this old grump. But I *was* joking about the swimming – just in case you were thinking of trying anything stupid! It's eleven miles of open water and it *is* the end of December!' Olive paused, watching Ivy carefully. 'You're *not* thinking of trying... are you?'

'Sharks!' said Mr Harris again.

Ivy let out an involuntary snort of laughter, making McGregor raise his head. Clearly, the little dog thought it was fine for him to snore, but woe betide anyone else if they made similar sounds!

'There must be a way to get off the island!' said Ivy. 'I need to get back to the mainland... to spend Christmas with my fiancé.'

The little white lie had slipped out for the second time before she could stop herself. But... so what that it wasn't strictly true? The fib was out there now and maybe it'd help her case a bit. It couldn't really hurt, could it? After all, once she was back on the mainland, it wasn't as though she'd ever see Olive or Mr Harris... or anyone else from the island ever again.

'Oh you poor lass,' said Olive, her face crumpling in sympathy.

A shock of pure guilt ran through Ivy – but it wasn't like she could undo the damage now, was it?

'When's the wedding?' asked Mr Harris abruptly.

'Erm...' said Ivy.

Uh oh! Suddenly this felt like it could take on a life of its own if she wasn't careful. Olive was watching her, looking interested. Right... in for a penny...

'We haven't set a date yet,' she said lowering her eyes and feeling a blush heat her face. 'He only asked me last night after we arrived.'

'Why's he not here with you then?' demanded Mr Harris. 'I don't know much about love and all that nonsense, but if I'd just put a ring on your finger lass, I wouldn't want to be more than a step away from you.'

Something in Ivy's heart melted at the gruff compliment, and she smiled at Mr Harris.

'You old dog!' laughed Olive.

'So where is he?' said Mr Harris again.

Blimey – an old dog with a bone!

'He wasn't feeling too hot this morning,' said Ivy. 'Service station food on the way up.'

'Oh dear – what a shame!' said Olive.

'Show us your sparkler, then!' said Mr Harris, leaning towards her slightly.

'Huh?' said Ivy.

'Your ring?' chuckled Olive. 'Let's see it!'

Damn! She hadn't thought of that small detail.

'Oh... I don't have it with me,' said Ivy quickly. 'He... I...'

Think, good woman, think!

'It's a beautiful vintage one – square cut sapphires and diamonds,' she said, quickly nicking her best friend Meg's proposal story. 'It belonged to his grandmother... but it's too big and I couldn't bear the idea of it slipping off in the cold so it's back in the m...' Ivy stuttered over the word "motel". That horrible hole didn't have a place in her perfect fantasy. 'It's back in the cottage,' she amended quickly.

'Ooh – you're staying in a little cottage?' asked Olive.

Ivy nodded. 'It's gorgeous. Two wood burners, sheepskin rugs, candles everywhere.'

'How romantic!' sighed Olive.

'Sounds like a fire hazard to me,' muttered Mr Harris, earning himself a playful swat from Olive.

'And how did he pop the question?' said Olive, her eyes shining.

'We were having a picnic in front of the fire – on a tartan blanket,' said Ivy, warming to her subject. It felt way too nice to put all her daydreams into words. 'The next thing I know he's on one knee and telling me that he can't live without me, and how the last two years have been perfect... and he's ready for marriage and children... and...'

'And...?' prompted Olive, her hand on her heart.

'And... he even said he'd iron his own underpants!' said Ivy, triumphantly.

'Erm... okay?!' said Olive looking surprised.

Oops! The real Gareth had just managed to sneak into her head to ruin her dream proposal - right as it was getting good too!

'One sec,' said Ivy, deciding that perhaps a change of subject might be in order before she managed to completely lose her audience, 'how's Jock getting home if the plane's not working?'

'You know,' said Mr Harris, 'technically, I think he's just the first officer.'

'Either way, Jock's fine' said Olive, 'he lives just up the road by loch Carey.'

'Oh,' said Ivy, her heart sinking again. So that was not such a great thought after all.

'You could try the ferry instead?' said Olive. 'I mean, it takes a lot longer, but you might just about get back this evening if you're lucky. It would probably be very late though.'

'No she can't,' said Mr Harris. 'It's in for its annual service, isn't it? It'll be in bits all over the boathouse - you mark my words!'

'Connor should be nearly finished by now, shouldn't he?' said Olive in surprise. 'It feels like he's been at it for days!'

Mr Harris simply shook his head and stared into his empty coffee cup.

CHRISTMAS ON CRUMCAREY

Ivy looked between them. Sure, it would take a lot longer than the flight, but at least it was transport! And she really did need to get back... as much as this had been fun, she wasn't really up for spending Christmas stranded on a remote island with a bunch of strangers and a wet dog. Especially as there was a good chance the dog in question might decide to savage her ankles at any moment.

'How do I get down to the harbour?' she asked.

'There's no po-oint,' Mr Harris crooned in a sing-song voice, making McGregor jump up and stare at him.

'Well - I've got to try!' said Ivy, taking advantage of her new-found dog-free state to get to her feet.

'It's easy,' said Olive. 'Go out the front door, turn left and head back towards the airport. Then go straight past the buildings there and follow the path on towards the harbour. You can't miss it...' she trailed off and looked Ivy up and down for a moment. 'Well, a local can't miss it!'

Mr Harris snorted with laughter and McGregor barked.

'I mean... I'm sure you've got some sense of direction,' said Olive, 'but if in doubt head towards the water and then look around for a great big shed. You'll find Connor inside. You can tell him I sent you.'

'And you can tell him I told you there was no point,' said Mr Harris.

'Oh hush!' chuckled Olive. 'The lass wants to get back to her man.'

Ivy smiled at her, feeling guilty – but there was no point worrying about that now. With any luck, this Connor would help her get back to reality.

'I'll give it a try,' said Ivy, doing her best to ignore the sound of the wind howling around the chimney. For a moment, she was tempted to sit straight back down, have another drink and just give in to the idea of staying put.

'Good luck!' said Olive. 'Don't forget your coat, you're going to need it!'

'Thank you for everything,' said Ivy, turning away from a beaming Olive and Mr Harris, who was shaking his head.

She'd just put her hand on the door to let herself into the porch when she remembered she still hadn't paid.

'Sorry!' said Ivy, turning back to the bar to find the pair of them still watching her intently. 'What do I owe you?'

Olive made a little ushering motion at her. 'Don't worry about that, dearie - you can pay me when you get back!'

Ivy hesitated for a second – after all, it wasn't exactly the most reassuring parting comment... but she was on a mission. Besides, she was sure she could always send the money to Olive when she got home. All she needed to do now was find a way back to

Gareth. That way, she could escape her little white lie that had somehow morphed into a full-blown romantic fantasy before she had to fess up to the fact that it was all wishful thinking. And – if she was going to get off the island, she needed to do it before it got dark.

Wrinkling her nose, Ivy pulled on her still-wet shoes and sodden coat. She buttoned it right up to the neck and yanked her hood into place while she was still under shelter. Then, taking a deep breath, Ivy headed back out into the rain.

CHAPTER 9

❄

It took precisely ten paces before Ivy started to regret her rash decision to brave the elements. Still – she wasn't one to be beaten by a bit of weather or a broken plane. She'd find this Connor person, get a plan in place and get back to Gareth in time for Christmas!

The rain had eased off a tiny bit since Ivy had made her dash from the airport to the Tallyaff, but not by much. Now – rather than heavy sheets of rain obscuring the view, there was a thick, almost misty curtain of drizzle doing the job instead. It was just wet enough to coat her eyelashes and force her to wipe her eyes every five seconds.

It only took ten minutes for Ivy to reach the airport buildings. Following Olive's instructions, she took the path towards the harbour and felt a strange sense of pride as it came into view ahead of her. Maybe her sense of direction wasn't *that* bad after all! That said... this really was a very small island!

The sight of the decidedly grouchy sea beyond the harbour mouth made Ivy pause for a moment. The waves were *huge!* No matter how determined she was to get a plan of action in place to leave Crumcarey... she didn't really like the idea of eleven miles worth of being bounced up and down on a boat!

'Man up!' she muttered into the rain. 'It's all part of the adventure!'

She'd worry about dealing with the mad, choppy sea later. First things first - she needed to find this Connor bloke and see if there was any chance of catching the ferry back to the mainland sometime today. If not... well, that *wasn't* an option. This *had* to work.

Just ahead of her a large, Ivy spotted a hand-painted sign that read "Ferry Terminal". It sounded rather grand, but in reality, the sign was nailed at a wonky angle to the side of a battered-looking boathouse. The place was made out of sheets of corrugated iron and bits of old wood. Ivy couldn't help but think that it was a bit of a miracle it hadn't been blown away. Even now, she could hear it creaking as gusts of wind hit it from all angles.

Over the groaning of the shed and the churning of the waves beyond, Ivy could just about make out the sound of hammering coming from the boatshed. Over the top of all this, there was a string of yelling in a language she couldn't quite make out... perhaps it was some kind of local dialect?

Ivy's stomach squeezed with nerves. What was this guy's name again? Connor – that was it. He didn't sound particularly friendly! Suddenly, Ivy wished she'd asked Olive a bit more about him. But no - she'd just rushed off into the rain in an attempt to escape her porkie pies about getting engaged.

Ivy winced at the memory. She had a feeling that moment was going to keep coming back to haunt her. She couldn't believe she'd lied and made Gareth out to be some kind of romantic hero... especially as he was basically the polar opposite.

Ah well, all the more reason to get on with her plan and get back to the mainland before she had to come clean! Ivy headed for the door, pausing briefly for another quick listen. The yelling had turned into a long string of muttering now, but she still couldn't make out the words - but it was obvious just by the tone that whatever was going on in there certainly wasn't going well.

There didn't seem to be much point knocking - there was no way anyone inside would be able to hear her. Ivy tugged at the door and was relieved to find that it wasn't locked. The scene that met her eyes made her heart sink.

Mr Harris had been right. There was a small, roll-on-roll-off ferry inside the boatshed. Actually, "small" wasn't really the right word - it was a pretty hefty beast

- but nothing like the huge ferry that had taken her across the channel to France a couple of years ago. This one looked like it could manage three or maybe four cars.

The size of the ferry wasn't what was bothering Ivy, though. It was the fact that most of its guts appeared to be anywhere other than where they should be. There were unidentified bits of engine-thingummybobs scattered around like there had been a minor explosion, and the main engine itself was currently hovering about ten feet in the air above the ferry. This was held in place by a thick chain that led to the arm of a squat little crane.

Right underneath this tonne of hovering metal, Ivy could just about make out a pair of legs and a bum clad in a pair of very dirty overalls. The top half of the figure was out of sight in the bowels of the boat, but she could still hear the mumbling string of curses drifting up from the hole.

Ivy wasn't quite sure what to do next. She didn't want to startle whoever belonged to those legs... not when he had his head inside a boat at quite such a precarious angle. Maybe if she just waited for a minute or two, he'd emerge under his own steam and realise he had an unexpected guest...?

Five minutes later, the guy in the overalls still hadn't emerged... and things didn't seem to be going any better for him either, given that he hadn't let up in the grumbling diatribe the entire time she'd been standing there.

This was getting silly! As far as Ivy could see, she had two choices. She could either turn tail and head back to the Tallyaff, or she could let this Connor bloke know she was here.

'Hello?'

She'd meant it to be a friendly call, but the word had crept out of her mouth like a frightened chipmunk – promptly disappearing under the creaking of the tin roof.

Pathetic!

Ivy cleared her throat and tried again.

'Hello!'

Her yell was met by the clatter of a tool being dropped, followed by a curse that was *definitely* in English this time.

'Who's there?' came a gruff voice from the direction of the legs… though no top half emerged.

'Erm… hi! I'm Ivy?'

'You don't sound very sure of that!' came the voice again.

'Oh. Well… hi!' said Ivy, taking a couple of tentative steps towards the legs.

'Ivy – I've no idea who you are, but right now's not a good time.'

'It'll only take a second!' she said, more bravely than she was feeling.

'Fine!' The word came out as a long-suffering growl. 'Give me a minute.'

Ivy watched as the legs and butt wriggled around, and then a grubby face appeared. The man was spitting curses out around a large screwdriver clenched between his teeth as he struggled into a sitting position to look at her.

Well, at least that explained one thing - it wasn't a strange local dialect she'd heard from outside after all, just the screwdriver getting in the way of all the Fs!

Ivy watched as the man took the screwdriver out of his mouth and laid it on the ground next to him. Then he stared back at her.

'Okay – I'm listening,' he said. 'What?!'

Ivy's jaw dropped and it took several seconds before she realised that she was gaping at him like a landed guppy – and not just because he was being so grumpy. This guy was... gorgeous. There was no other word for it. Even covered in grease and wearing a pair of overalls that looked like they might be wide enough to fit five of him in.

'He-llo?!' he demanded, looking pissed off. 'I'm a bit busy here?!'

'Sorry... sorry...' gasped Ivy, now completely unable to look away from the pair of bright blue eyes that had her pinned. 'I'm Ivy.'

'Yeah... you said that already,' the man sighed. 'I'm Conner. What do you want, Ivy?'

'I was wondering if you could help me get back to the mainland,' she said.

'Help you get back to the mainland?' said Connor with a frown.

'The plane isn't working,' she said, feeling more than a little bit stupid.

'Well, you're stuck on the island then,' he said, wiping his hands on the front of his overalls. 'I'd suggest you book your Christmas dinner at the Tallyaff. It's very popular.'

'Nope,' said Ivy. She could feel a kind of grumpy determination steeling up on her. She had a plan, and she was going to damn well make it happen. 'I intend to leave this island as soon as possible and spend Christmas with my fiancé back on the mainland.'

Even as she said it, Ivy couldn't help but think that she sounded like a total prat. Not to mention that it was a stunningly bad idea to wheel out her little fantasy life for another airing!

'Well Ivy, it's like this,' said the Conner. 'If the plane is broken, then they will have to order parts. To get the parts here, they need to bring them in by ferry. This is the ferry, and it's currently undergoing its annual maintenance and service.'

'Can't you just…?' started Ivy.

'No!' growled Connor. 'I *can't just!* I have been awake for the last twenty-nine hours getting that bloody engine out. It will take me just as long to get it back in because it's being a right-' Connor paused and took a deep breath before continuing. 'Nuisance,' he said carefully. 'When that's done - and not before - I will sail off into the very rough Christmassy sea and go and fetch parts for the plane. But until then you're stuck because - as you can see - the ferry is out of service at the moment.'

Ivy stared as Connor turned away from her and muttered something along the lines of *bloody tourists* before placing the screwdriver back in his mouth and lowering his head back into the depths of the ferry.

'Oh,' whispered Ivy, not quite knowing how to react. 'Okay... I'll just go then.'

She turned and began picking her way through the various bits of boat on the way to the door. She'd almost reached it when there was a strange ripping sound behind her followed by renewed and much more urgent sounding swearing.

'Are... are you okay?' she called.

'Ivy? Are you still there?!' he shouted, sounding really grumpy now

'Sorry... I'll go!' said Ivy, hurrying towards the door.

'No... NO!'

Ivy turned back again, but she didn't dare say anything.

'I...erm... I appear to be stuck.'

Ivy felt her eyes grow wide.

'Can you... give me a hand?'

For a very brief second, Ivy hesitated. After all... the guy was decidedly rude. But then she relented. The poor bloke was clearly having a bad day... and she knew how that felt!

Ivy hurried back to his side and crouched next to him.

'What's up?' she said.

'These damn overalls,' came Connor's voice, sounding strained from his awkward angle dangling over the ferry. 'They're so bloody big they've got hooked on something!'

Ivy had to bite her lip to stop herself from laughing.

'They're caught on something around my waist somewhere!' said Connor.

'Okay – let me look,' said Ivy, holding out her hand and then pausing awkwardly as she realised that she was going to have to feel around underneath him. Well... there was nothing for it! 'Don't jump – I'm going to see if I can unhook you!'

Doing her best to keep her mind out of the gutter as her hands traced around either side of Connor's waist, Ivy tugged at the voluminous overalls, trying to figure out where they were stuck.

'Erm,' she said, glad he couldn't see her flaming face, 'can you shift your weight a bit to your left?'

Connor grunted and wriggled, and Ivy let her hands trace the fabric underneath him. She did her best to ignore the warm, hard body she could feel under the oily overalls.

'Got it!' she said, her voice sounding thick in her ears. 'One of the pockets is caught on a hook!'

With some difficulty, Ivy wiggled the torn fabric until it came free. 'Okay – you should be able to move now!' she said, scooting back away from him so that she didn't get trampled as he hauled himself back into a sitting position.

'You okay?' she asked after he'd sat there staring at her in silence for a full minute.

Connor nodded. 'Yeah. Erm… thank you.'

Ivy watched as he clambered to his feet. It was no wonder he'd got stuck – the overalls he was wearing were about five sizes too large for him – at least width-ways.

Catching her staring, Connor glanced down at them, sticking a finger into the hole he'd just managed to rip next to the offending pocket. He pulled a face.

'Mr McCluskey will have my guts for garters – these are his favourites!' he sighed, before shrugging out of the top half of them and tying the sleeves firmly around his waist.

Ivy swallowed. Underneath the grubby overalls, Connor was wearing a surprisingly clean white tee shirt. The soft cotton did nothing to hide the fact that the man was basically solid muscle. That wasn't the only thing that had just rendered Ivy completely mute, though. Connor's arms were covered in tattoos, the dark ink snaking out from beneath the white cotton and trailing in curling, Celtic knotwork all the way down to his wrists.

Ivy swallowed again, her mouth dry.

CHRISTMAS ON CRUMCAREY

'Look,' said Connor, his voice much softer now, 'I'm sorry if I was a bit of a prat just now. It feels like I've been working at this for days... and I've had far too much coffee and hardly anything to eat.'

'Don't worry about it,' muttered Ivy, trying to tear her eyes away from Connor's arms. 'Sounds like your day is going as well as mine!'

'For what it's worth, I'm sorry about the ferry!' said Connor.

Ivy shrugged. After all, it wasn't like it was his fault.

'I understand... you wanting to get back to your fiancé, and all,' said Connor.

Ivy winced. Damn it – so he'd heard that bit, had he? She *really* needed to get off of Crumcarey before she booked a venue for the non-existent wedding! 'What about those fishing boats I saw in the harbour?' she said. 'Could one of them take me over?'

'All the fishermen are on holiday,' said Connor. 'Mr McCluskey has gone to Greece with his wife and I think Terry Livingstone is in the Maldives. They won't be back until the New Year. They like to spend a couple of weeks warming up every year... I can't say I blame them!' he added with a laugh as the wind chose that moment to set the roof of the shed clattering again.

Ivy felt her last hope of getting back for Christmas blowing away with the gusts.

'Now then...' said Connor, frowning in concern as he watched her face fall, 'don't look like that! We're not that bad, you know!'

'Please, can't you help me?' said Ivy. She knew she sounded small and pathetic and not at all like herself… but she couldn't help it. Right now, it felt like her entire life was shifting out of control, and she wasn't sure she liked it.

'Look,' said Connor, 'I'll see what I can do.'

And then he smiled.

Ivy's knees promptly turned to jelly. Oh hell… a smile like that shouldn't be allowed anywhere near someone who'd just realised her relationship was probably over.

CHAPTER 10

❄

Ivy trudged back towards the Tallyaff, enjoying the cool drizzle as it soothed her burning cheeks. Every time she blinked, there seemed to be an image of Connor's strong, tattooed arms burned in the back of her eyelids.

Bloody hell!

She'd just have to keep reminding herself what a grumpy sod he clearly was... only... he wasn't, was he? After she'd saved him from the killer overalls, he'd actually been quite sweet... in a sleep-deprived, stressed kind of way! But what did it matter *what* Connor was really like?!

Ivy shook her head, cross with herself. The only thing that mattered right now was that the guy had given her a tiny glimmer of hope to cling to. He'd said that he'd try to get the engine back into the ferry so that he could take her back to the mainland in time for

Christmas Day – or at least, maybe first thing in the morning.

Given that it had taken him twenty-nine hours to remove the engine in the first place, it was an incredibly sweet offer, but Ivy wasn't going to hold her breath. Besides, he'd probably just said it to get rid of her!

Ivy stopped dead, bracing against yet another gust of fierce island wind. She really *had* to stop doing that! Just because Gareth was always telling her she was in the way, or bugging him, or irritating him in some way shape or form – it didn't mean everyone else found her quite so annoying.

In fact, as she stared in the direction of the Tallyaff, doing her best to spot its stone walls through the rain, Ivy couldn't help but wonder why she was trying so hard to get back to Gareth anyway.

The realisation she'd just had in the boatshed – the one she'd been desperately trying to ignore - echoed around her head again. Was she right? Were things over between them?

Well… she had to admit one thing to herself. The way her body was still reeling from thirty seconds of contact with Connor was about a million miles away from the way she reacted to Gareth. Or - if she was being *completely* honest – had *ever* reacted to Gareth.

Ivy took a deep breath and set off again as the truth continued to punch her in the head and heart. She knew she couldn't blame everything on this disastrous trip. After all, things had been going downhill for months. Now, though, it had reached the point where just thinking about Gareth made her ball her fists up in anger. That couldn't be right, could it?

There was one thing troubling her above everything else. Ivy had been waiting for Gareth to propose for ages. Would she *really* have said yes if he'd asked? Suddenly, the idea of being stuck with that decision for the rest of her life was enough to terrify her.

Ivy could see that she'd been holding on so tightly to the perfect fantasy of her and Gareth, that she'd managed to avoid facing the reality for far too long. They were horrible together – and she needed to do something about it.

Right now, though, Ivy had to admit that she was stressed and over-caffeinated. Perhaps it might be best to leave the big decisions that would affect the rest of her life until she was a bit calmer. But... something was whispering in her ear that this trip to Crumcarey might be some kind of cosmic intervention. It felt a bit like the universe had stepped in, given her a great big festive slap across the face, and yelled at her to wake up... and when the universe did things like that, it was usually a good idea to listen.

Right now, there were three things Ivy knew for certain – and she was going to cling to them for dear life. Number one - she wasn't engaged. Number two – she'd just met a man who had the ability to turn her knees to jelly with a simple smile. Number three – she was now soaked to the skin and freezing. It was time to get back to the Tallyaff sharpish, before she was quite literally swept off her feet – and not in the way she'd been hoping.

❄

By the time Ivy got back to the guest house, Mr Harris had barely moved. He was still chatting away at the bar with Olive. McGregor got to his feet and trotted towards her, wagging his tail like she was a long-lost friend.

Ivy froze. Wasn't this dog meant to be vicious towards strangers? He stopped right in front of her, still wagging madly.

'I see you didn't try to swim then?' said Olive, smiling as Ivy did her best to wipe as much of the rain from her face as she could with her damp sleeve.

'No way I'd brave those waves!' laughed Ivy.

'Because of the sharks!' said Mr Harris.

Ivy looked from Mr Harris to Olive and then back again.

'He *is* joking, right?' said Ivy. 'There aren't *really* sharks, are there?!'

'He's just pulling your leg,' said Olive. 'There aren't any sharks. Well... there are, but not the dangerous type. You'd probably bump into some jellyfish, though. Most of them aren't too bad... but you don't want to mess with the little purple ones. The problem is, you can't see them coming because they're under the water... so what colour they are doesn't really enter into it until you feel the sting!'

'No more jellyfish,' said Mr Harris. 'All gone.'

'Oh no they're not!' said Olive, making Ivy feel like she'd just landed in the middle of a pantomime.

'Oh yes they are,' retorted Mr Harris with a grin. 'Sharks ate them all.'

With that, he got to his feet with some difficulty and gathered his sticks. Then, he clicked his fingers at McGregor, who promptly trotted over and followed the old man's heel as he headed towards the door at a slow shuffle.

'I'll be off home now. See you tomorrow. Merry Christmas,' he said. 'Enjoy your stay,' he added, turning to wink at Ivy.

Before Ivy could reply, he'd disappeared through the door with McGregor hot on his heels.

'I'm sorry about Mr Harris,' laughed Olive. 'He's got a bit of a strange sense of humour. Still - he does have a point, it *does* look like you might be staying the night... unless you had any success with Connor?'

'I'm not sure about success,' said Ivy, doing her best not to blush at the mention of his name. 'I did find him though.'

'And?' prompted Olive.

'He was a bit...' she paused.

She couldn't quite think of the best way to describe

him. Lots of words were coming to mind. Grumpy. Gorgeous. Oily and practically edible…

'He was a bit…' she started again, '…over-tired, I think.' She quickly decided not to mention anything about the overall incident and having to help free him. It didn't seem fair to go spreading that around the island! 'He did say that he's going to try to get the engine back in the ferry so that he can get me back to the mainland. Either today or maybe tomorrow morning. But… it took him twenty-nine hours to get the thing out… so… I'm guessing he's joking?'

'If Connor says he's going to try to do something, he means it,' said Olive. 'Though how on earth he's going to pull this one off is beyond me!'

Ivy nodded in agreement. Maybe there wasn't any harm in booking a room. Considering her luck on this trip so far, she had a feeling she was going to need it!

'Olive, do you have a room to spare?' she said, crossing her fingers. 'I know it's Christmas, but…?'

'Don't you worry about that,' said Olive with a smile. 'I've got just the room for you. Should I put it on your tab?'

❄

Ten minutes later, Ivy was trudging wearily up the stairs in search of her room. There were no new-fangled swipe cards for the doors here at the Tallyaff. Instead, she was clutching the chunkiest key she'd ever seen. It was attached to a large wooden fob with the room number painted on it. There was no chance she'd be losing this bad boy! In fact, she was pretty sure she could use it as ballast next time she had to go outside - with this in her pocket there'd be no chance of her blowing away.

Olive had put her in room 307. Ivy grinned. She was pretty certain there weren't over three hundred rooms at the Tallyaff. Probably more like two dozen at a push. But as she wandered along the first-floor hallway, she noticed that each room had a completely random number assigned to it, ranging from zero to ten thousand... and as far as Ivy could tell, they weren't in any particular order either.

Luckily, Olive had given her directions on how to get to room 307. Ivy hadn't really taken them in the first time around – she'd been too busy daydreaming about grabbing a shower. She wasn't expecting too much from the room, but as long as it had hot, running water, she didn't really care how basic it was! Noticing that Ivy was away with the fairies, Olive had repeated the directions to the room slowly and clearly, making sure that she was focusing. At the time, Ivy'd thought it was overkill – but now she could see why Olive had done it!

At long last, Ivy wound her way around yet another corner – having passed rooms 2 and 5098 - only to come face to face with room 307.

'Yay!'

Ivy's cheer was more than a little bit weary. She needed to sit down before she fell down. All that wind and salty sea air had absolutely wiped her out.

With a slow, almost defeated movement, Ivy slotted the key into the lock, turned it and pushed her way inside.

'Oh my goodness!' she breathed.

The room was absolutely massive. Painted in soft eggshell colours, it was illuminated by strings of dainty Christmas lights that wound their way down the four posts of the bed and along the back of an elegant dressing table.

Stepping inside, Ivy flicked the main light switch and various lamps around the room sprang to life, filling the shadows with a rosy glow.

The window opposite the door looked out towards the sea, and light from the lamps glittered off golden seed pods that Olive had used in a festive dried-flower display that sat in an old glass bottle on the sill.

Ivy moved towards the ginormous bed and ran her hand along the covers. There were at least three duvets, topped with a cosy tartan cashmere blanket. It was too inviting to resist, and Ivy let herself topple onto the bed, letting out a sigh of pure pleasure. It was firm yet decidedly squishy, just the way she liked it. It couldn't be further from the horrible mattress at the motel – all thin and limp, with a trench right down the middle full of broken springs that had tortured her into the early hours of the morning.

Ivy wriggled around and stared at the room again, unable to believe her luck. The Tallyaff just kept getting better and better. This room almost made up for missing out on the cosy cottage – it was clean and bright and had a lovely, friendly feeling to it.

Turning to stare out of the window, Ivy was momentarily blinded as a beam of golden sunlight pierced the rainclouds. Two seconds later, she watched as it disappeared over the horizon and darkness fell as quickly as if someone had flipped a switch out there.

'Wow!' said Ivy. Well, that was the end of the daylight then - she'd had no idea that it was already that late in the afternoon!

For a brief second, Ivy felt her stress levels start to climb again. This wasn't good, was it? There was no way anyone was going to get her back to the mainland now! Was there any chance that Connor might get the ferry back in one piece this evening? If he did, would he take it out in the dark? She somehow doubted it.

Tomorrow was Christmas day. It looked like she was officially stuck here until the morning... she couldn't get back to Gareth.

Ivy flopped back onto the pillows, breathing deeply for a moment as she willed herself to calm down. Then, just like a cork shooting out of a champagne bottle, all the tension disappeared from her body with one short, sharp laugh.

CHAPTER 11

❄

*N*ow she'd given in to the fact that she was likely to spend at least one night here at the Tallyaff, Ivy decided that it was time to investigate the room properly. After all, she might as well enjoy it!

Untangling herself from the cosy mound of bedding, Ivy shuffled her way across the room to check out what she *hoped* would be the ensuite. She wasn't about to assume anything after her experience back at the motel!

'Don't be a cupboard... don't be a cupboard!' she chanted, slowly opening the door while resisting the temptation to close her eyes.

'Bingo!' she cheered as a pile of fluffy towels came into view. They were nestling on top of an old bentwood chair. There was a cosy robe folded over the back too, complete with a pair of fluffy slippers sitting underneath.

As if that wasn't a promising enough start, the sight that met Ivy's eyes as she wandered inside almost reduced her to a quivering wreck of happy tears. There was a huge, gleaming, claw-footed bath sitting there as if it had been waiting for her. It was official, she was in heaven.

There was a little wooden trolley beside the bath with rows of mini-soaps and bottles of shampoo, conditioner, moisturiser and all the delicious smellies a girl could ask for. Their gorgeous, blue glass bottles twinkled in the light, ready to turn bath time into a feast for the senses.

Ivy picked up a bottle of body lotion, snapped the seal and opened it to take a sniff. Clouds of lavender and rose tickled her senses and threatened to intoxicate her. Well – she had to hand it to Olive – she certainly had good taste!! She couldn't wait to wallow in the deepest, longest bubble bath imaginable without Gareth barging in just as she was starting to relax.

The rogue thought of Gareth instantly took Ivy straight back to the horrific bathroom situation at the motel. It had boasted a grubby half-bath ringed with thick bands of other people's dead skin. The shower cubicle hadn't been much cleaner, but she'd decided that was the lesser of two evils. She'd had to dash along the hallway wrapped in a towel that was so thin and crusty it hadn't wanted to bend. When she'd ventured in, intent on washing away the grime of the long, boring journey, she'd promptly come face to face with an old bar of half-used soap. The cherry on top had been the curl of dark, wiry hair embedded in its surface.

Ivy shuddered. Perhaps if she stared at the giant, gleaming tub in front of her hard enough, she'd be able to wipe that grimy image from her memory completely.

Right - there was one last thing she needed to check before this bathroom won a gold star...

Stepping forward, Ivy turned the huge tap and held her breath. There was a brief, loud burble as the pipes considered whether to play ball or not and then a stream of scolding hot water started to splash into the bath. That settled it – this was the most amazing room she'd ever had the pleasure of staying in.

Ivy quickly turned the tap back off again. As much as she'd love nothing more right now than to sink under a fluffy layer of bubbles – she had something far less pleasant she needed to do first.

Giving the glorious tub a longing, backward glance, Ivy headed back into the bedroom. Eyeballing the bed longingly, she let out a huge yawn. Suddenly, she was absolutely exhausted - she hadn't managed to get much sleep the night before what with the murder-springs and the constant dog-waffle coming from Gareth's direction. Add to that the epic drive the entire length of Britain... it wasn't really surprising that it was all catching up with her!

Ivy stretched and let out another yawn.

At least she didn't have to spend the evening trying to get an engine back inside a ferry like poor Connor! If anyone needed a catnap on a soft, tartan blanket she had a feeling it was him. He'd looked dead on his feet earlier... and now she felt a bit guilty for adding to that by basically begging the poor guy to come to her rescue.

Maybe she should go back down to the boatshed in a little while and see how he was doing. Perhaps she could take him a couple of Olive's pastries and a coffee to keep him going. Actually, scratch that... he said that he'd already had too much coffee... perhaps it would be better just to leave him to get on with it. Gareth always hated it when she tried to do anything like that. In fact, he always used it as an excuse to get in a huff and abandon whatever he was trying to do and leave stuff scattered everywhere for a week.

'Yeah well... if you'd have just let me get on with it without poking your nose in, I'd have finished it!'

Ivy balled her fist and fought back the urge to growl.

'Calm down, idiot!' she said. It probably wasn't the best plan to get herself in a grump with him right now... not when the time had come to finally call him.

Ivy crossed to where she'd dumped her handbag and rummaged around for her phone. A sudden spike of guilt ran through her. She should have been on the return flight back to the mainland hours ago. Poor

Gareth would be worried – she should have called him sooner!

Praying that she still had plenty of charge, Ivy flicked the phone on.

'Huh!'

There wasn't a single missed call or message. Maybe there wasn't any signal?

Full signal.

So… she'd disappeared on a flight to a remote island… failed to reappear when she was meant to… and he hadn't even bothered to send her a *text?!*

It was official – she needed to chill out a bit before she called him, otherwise a few too many home truths were going to come spilling out the minute he answered the phone!

Rather than standing around fuming, Ivy flopped extravagantly onto the bed and did a few little starfish movements like she was trying to create snow angels in the mound of duvets. It worked a treat – she was grinning like a lunatic within seconds… though that was mostly down to the fact that she'd just realised that she'd get the entire bed to herself that night!

Right, it was time to call Gareth. Frankly, it was the last thing Ivy wanted to do, but she knew she had to. Even if he was an uncaring, thoughtless plonker, she didn't want to be one too! Still, it took every ounce of determination she could muster not to hang up while she waited for him to pick up.

'What?'

Gareth's voice made Ivy flinch. He always answered the phone in the same way, unless he was expecting a call from his mother and he wanted to fleece her for a top-up of his perma-empty bank account. Then he tended to be a little bit more polite. Not a *lot* more polite, but at least a little bit.

'Hi,' said Ivy.

'Oh, it's you,' said Gareth, sounding huffy.

Well, there was a warm welcome for you!

Wasn't he at least the tiniest bit worried about her?

'What do you want?' he said.

'Well,' said Ivy, doing her best to keep her voice steady, 'there's been a bit of a problem with the plane.'

'You should have listened to me, shouldn't you?' said Gareth, sounding smug.

'Huh?' said Ivy.

'You should have stayed with me at the motel. I *told* you I didn't want you going!'

Ivy rolled her eyes, suddenly glad that they weren't on a video call. Normally, she'd just start agreeing with him to keep the peace... but not this time. She'd had enough of being the one to smooth everything over.

'You know,' she said, 'this whole trip was your idea in the first place!'

'I just knew that something like this was going to happen,' Gareth continued, clearly not listening to a word she'd just said.

Ivy pursed her lips and did her best not to start grinding her teeth. Gareth often talked like he was some kind of fortune teller. It was nothing new... but right now, the temptation to hit the big, red "end call" button was almost overwhelming.

As she listened to Gareth warming up to how all this was *'all her fault,'* Ivy felt her shoulders heading rapidly towards her earlobes. Suddenly, she desperately wanted to punch something. Fortunately, there was currently eleven miles of shark-infested water between her and the *something* she wanted to punch. All she could do for now was twist her fingers into the fluffy duvet like she was trying to wring its neck.

Ivy had always known that Gareth could have a bad effect on her mood. She had ignored it for a long time - plastering the cracks with a fantasy version of their relationship... a fantasy version of Gareth! That was the simple truth. As she caught the dreaded words "dog" and "training classes" – Ivy finally had to admit to herself that she'd been in a two-year relationship with a figment of her imagination.

The real mystery was how the pair of them had managed to stay together for so long without things coming to a head?

Still, she wasn't a monster. Ivy knew what needed to be done – but it wasn't something that they could be done over the phone... especially not on Christmas Eve!

'Look,' said Ivy, realising that she hadn't said a word in about three minutes. 'I've spoken to the guy who runs the ferry, and he's trying to get it working again so I can get back over to you.'

'I thought you said it was the plane that was broken,' said Gareth in a suspicious tone.

'It is,' said Ivy with a sigh. 'I thought I might be able to catch the ferry back instead, but it's out of the water for its annual maintenance.'

'That place sounds awful,' huffed Gareth.

'It's really not,' said Ivy, a little smile escaping her as the image of Connor stripping off the top half of his overalls popped into her head.

Oops! Maybe not the time for that particular daydream!

'Anyway,' said Ivy, giving her head a quick shake. 'The plane is broken and the ferry is as good as broken.'

She paused again. There really wasn't any point going into the details with Gareth. Even if he *was* listening – which was highly unlikely - he didn't really understand how things worked. Toasters. Kettles. Washing machines. The man was flummoxed by a simple on-off switch.

'Isn't there someone there with a boat who could bring you back over?' said Gareth. His voice had now taken on its customary, sulky tone.

'Apparently, all the fishermen are on holiday somewhere warm and exotic,' she said.

Somewhere like he should have taken her for their Christmas holidays - instead of a cheap, nasty motel.

Ivy didn't say this out loud though - no matter how

much she wanted to. She couldn't be bothered getting into a fight with him right now.

'You could always swim back,' said Gareth.

Ivy took a moment to absorb the idiocy of what he'd just said. When Olive and Mr Harris had suggested it earlier, they'd been joking – trying to lighten the mood and make her laugh. Gareth *wasn't* joking. Still, thanks to her new friends, she had the perfect answer ready for him.

'Are you kidding?' she said. 'It's eleven miles - and it's December - and there are sharks!'

'Now you're just being silly,' said Gareth.

'Well, you started it,' said Ivy, her determination to remain calm suddenly giving way.

'So, what am I supposed to do?' said Gareth. 'Some Christmas I'm going to have, all on my own in this place!'

Ivy blinked slowly.

This was *typical* Gareth. He never thought about anyone other than himself. She'd disappeared on a flight on Christmas Eve and hadn't returned... and he either hadn't noticed or hadn't cared. And now that he knew she was going to be stranded for Christmas, his only concern was for himself.

'You'll just have to entertain yourself, won't you?!' said Ivy tersely. 'I've done my best – there's nothing else I can do.'

'But we still need to talk about the dog thing,' whined Gareth. 'I've been thinking about it. As you're being so unreasonable, I guess I don't mind doing the morning walks - but only sometimes. Not all the time. If that helps.'

Ivy silently started to count to ten. She knew that Gareth was expecting her to say something like "I'm thinking about it" – which to him meant the same as "yes". Not this time, though. This time she kept her mouth firmly shut. She was tired. It was almost Christmas and she didn't want to be on the phone with him anymore.

She was here at the lovely Tallyaff and she was warm and comfortable. Despite the seismic shifts that were on their way... Ivy felt stirrings of happiness somewhere deep in her soul.

Even so, this wasn't the moment for *that* conversation. Ivy really didn't want to end a two-year relationship over the phone. She might be cross with Gareth – but she wasn't heartless. Still... it didn't mean she had to listen to any more of his crap, did it?!

'Merry Christmas,' she muttered, and promptly hung up.

Well, that was that, then!

Ivy snuggled down into the pillows, cocooned in a nest of fluffy duvets. She wasn't sure how it happened, but before she had a chance to think about what a total lemon she'd been for wasting almost two years of her life with a self-obsessed idiot... before she'd even managed to trace the first tear as it trickled down her cheek... she fell fast asleep.

CHAPTER 12

※

Ivy's eyes felt sticky and caked together. Giving them a rub, she let out an extravagant yawn before staring around her in confusion. For a split second, she was completely unable to figure out where she was. This certainly wasn't the awful motel... the bed was far too comfortable... and there was no sign of Gareth!

Just the thought of him was enough to bring everything rushing back. Ivy was rolled in a cocoon of cosy duvets in a guest house on a tiny island in the middle of nowhere.

And... there was a very good chance that she might have just managed to sleep right the way through Christmas day. Oops!

Sitting bolt upright, she stared towards the window and sighed with relief. It was still dark outside. She'd either slept for twenty-four hours straight, or it was still Christmas Eve - just a little bit further into Christmas Eve than she'd been expecting. Ivy quickly grabbed her phone – just to double-check. Yep! Christmas Eve. And right there, waiting for her, was a text from Gareth.

Ivy's heart gave a little squeeze, and she felt herself soften. Poor Gareth, maybe she'd been a bit harsh on him earlier. She tapped her screen.

"Suppose you lost signal. You could have called me back. We need to get this dog situation ironed out, Ivy. I'm seriously upset that you're not taking my needs seriously. I expect you back here tomorrow morning, otherwise I'm taking the car and going home. G."

'Bog off, knobhead!' growled Ivy, hitting the power button before tossing the phone away from her. It bounced across the mattress and disappeared under the tartan blanket. Well – that's what she got for a few seconds of remorse!

Urgh!

This meant she was going to have to find out what was going on with the ferry as soon as possible. The last thing she really wanted to do was put any more pressure on Connor than she already had, but Gareth wasn't giving her much choice in the matter. Knowing him, that wasn't an empty threat – she knew that he was more than capable of leaving her stranded in Scotland.

Heaving herself to her feet, Ivy gave the bed a sad farewell pat. So much for treating herself to a nice, long bath before heading back downstairs. Still, there would be time to wallow in bubbles later. Right now, her priority had to be getting herself back to the mainland.

❄

'Hello dearie!' said Olive, smiling at her from her perch behind the bar.

'Hi!' said Ivy, returning the smile and then peering around the room. It was still empty of customers. The curtains had been drawn, but she could hear the rain beating against the windowpanes and the wind whistling around the chimney.

Thankfully, the wood burner was still roaring, and the place was gorgeously warm and cosy. One thing was for sure – even if Connor *had* managed to get the ferry up and running, it would take a pack of wild dogs to drag her out into that storm this evening!

'Everything okay with your room?' asked Olive.

Ivy nodded, turning to her. 'It's gorgeous, thank so mu...' she trailed off. She hadn't realised there was anyone else in here, but her eyes had just fixed on a figure at the far end of the bar.

'Is that Connor?' she hissed, her voice dropping to a whisper as she padded over towards Olive. Ivy didn't really need an answer – it was *obvious* it was

Connor. She could see the tattoos snaking up his arms.

Looking slightly less grubby now that he'd removed his huge overalls, Connor was slumped forwards – barely balancing on his bar stool. He had one hand wrapped around a pint of beer and the other one was acting as a pillow between his face and the bar!

'Can I get you anything?' said Olive in a low voice, clearly not wanting to disturb him.

Ivy shook her head, still frowning at Connor. She couldn't believe it! The guy had promised her that he'd do everything he could to get the ferry fixed so that he could take her back… but here he was, drunk and comatose.

'Food?' persisted Olive, 'drink?'

Ivy did her best to stop scowling as she tore her eyes away from Connor's peaceful face to look at Olive… who was biting her lip, clearly having a great deal of trouble keeping a straight face.

'*What?!*' demanded Ivy, meeting the older woman's eyes.

'Poor lad – you'll set him on fire if you keep glaring at him like that!' said Olive.

'Yeah… well…' huffed Ivy.

'He did his best, dearie,' said Olive. 'He came straight here as soon as he knew.'

'Knew what?' said Ivy. 'That he needed a drink?!'

'Knew that there was no way he was going to manage to get the job done in time for tomorrow,' said Olive. 'It didn't matter how hard or fast he worked – the poor love was exhausted. It wouldn't have been safe - trying to do it on his own.' She paused, her cheerful face looking slightly stern for a brief moment. 'He felt really bad, you know.'

'Oh,' said Ivy, feeling herself deflate. 'Well, I guess that pint he's clutching is on me, then.'

'He was so tired, he ordered that drink then fell fast asleep before he even took one sip,' said Olive, smiling over at him.

Suddenly, Ivy felt awful. She'd jumped straight to the wrong conclusion... and she knew exactly why. After almost two years with Gareth, assuming the worst of people had become her default setting.

Poor old Connor wasn't drunk, just absolutely exhausted from doing his best to get her back to civilisation in time for Christmas with her imaginary fiancé. Not that she should really count the motel as civilisation!

Ivy let out a long sigh, making Olive giggle.

'So, can I get you anything?' she said, with an extravagant gesture to the array of bottles and gleaming optics behind the bar. 'It's Christmas, after all!'

Other than the occasional glass of wine, Ivy didn't drink very often. But... like Olive had just said... it *was*

Christmas. She might as well get into the spirit of things!

Spirit being the operative word.

Ivy eyeballed the row of scotch bottles with interest.

'Uh oh!' said Olive.

Ivy grinned at her, a naughty gleam in her eye as she pointed to one at random.

'I'd like one of those, please,' she said.

Olive gave her an approving nod.

'And can you put it on my tab, along with the room and anything else Connor wants when he wakes up?' she said. 'I've decided to stay.'

'Oh, you have, have you?' chuckled Olive as she poured Ivy a generous measure and placed it on the bar next to her. 'And - of course you can, it's our pleasure to have you here.'

Ivy picked up the glass of amber liquid and tilted it in the light before taking a long sniff. This was nothing like the rough stuff she'd tried when she was a teenager. This smelled smoky and peaty... and wonderful. So wonderful that Ivy could swear she was tipsy on that little sniff alone.

Under Olive's watchful eye, Ivy brought the glass to her lips and took a sip.

'Good eh?!' said Olive with a wink.

Ivy nodded. It had slipped down a treat – all smooth, velvety and earthy - it tasted a bit like Christmas.

As a trickle of fire warmed her throat and bloomed in her belly, Ivy had a fleeting thought that it might be a good idea to ask for something to eat. After all, those pastries had been quite a long time ago, and they weren't going to be man enough to help soak up something this strong.

Ah well... maybe later. There was no hurry, was there? Connor was still snoozing on the bar, and the room was golden and warm around her. Ivy could think of much worse ways to spend Christmas Eve. She took another long, slow sip of whiskey.

❄

There was definitely some kind of deja vu happening here on Crumcarey. Ivy cracked her sticky eyes open and stretched. Two seconds later, her entire body grumbled in protest. Urgh... had she come down with the flu or something? She certainly felt clammy enough!

Ivy peered around in confusion. The sliver of light from beneath the bedroom curtain threatened to drill a hole in her brain. She was desperately trying to figure out two things - where was she? And why did she feel like she'd been hit by a flying reindeer?

The *where* was easy enough to answer after she'd taken a second to gather her wits. She was back up in her room at the Tallyaff, stretched out on her bed. Only, this time around she didn't feel quite so comfortable. She was pinned underneath three duvets – and from what she could tell, she was still fully dressed. At least that explained the sticky, clammy heat! She wriggled around and kicked the covers onto the floor. It took a surprising amount of effort.

The second question - *why* she felt quite so hideous - was proving a bit more difficult to answer. She wracked her brains - something that felt decidedly uncomfortable. The last thing she remembered was talking to Gareth and then hanging up on him... and then having a nap? Had she just been plagued by strange dreams?

Hmm... no... there were other memories after that... if she could get them to stop wibbling in and out of focus long enough to get hold of them properly...

Gareth's text! Of course. She'd gone downstairs... and... oh crap! Maybe she didn't want to remember after all! Then, perhaps she could convince herself that she hadn't made a full-frontal attack on Olive's whisky selection!

Sitting up with a groan, Ivy waited for the room to stop spinning. Okay... so, that wasn't going to happen. Maybe if it could just slow down a bit, that'd be an excellent start. She tugged at her tee shirt, which had rucked up and was currently attempting to throttle her.

Ivy needed water... coffee... and paracetamol.

She felt grubby and disgusting. She'd never actually managed to make it into the luxurious bath yesterday. Maybe a quick shower would be a good idea. She definitely needed one... but there was something much more urgent to do first given the disturbing images that were flashing into her head right now.

Had she told some random stranger that she loved him?

And... had there been some kind of dancing?

Ivy rubbed her eyes wearily. First things first – she had to find out exactly what kind of trouble she'd managed to get herself into last night. She needed to go downstairs and find Olive. With any luck, there wouldn't be anyone else around yet. Then, if everything was as bad as she had a *very nasty* feeling it might be, she could come back up here and wallow in a bath until the New Year arrived.

After successfully sneaking down the stairs without bumping into a living soul, Ivy crept into the main room and breathed a sigh of relief. Olive was the only one around – perched at the bar and preparing a humungous bowl of brussels sprouts with a viciously sharp little knife.

'Merry Christmas!' she boomed, spotting Ivy and treating her to a huge grin.

Ivy returned the smile, wincing as Olive's jolly greeting grabbed her hangover by the neck and gave it a good shake.

'Oh dear,' laughed Olive, eyeballing her less-than-festive face. 'One sec dearie, I'll sort you out.'

Before Ivy could say anything, Olive had put down her knife and disappeared into the kitchen. Ivy perched on one of the barstools and sank forwards, resting her elbows on the wood and burying her face in her hands.

'Here!' said Olive, about five minutes later.

Ivy peeped through her fingers. The sight of a chunky bacon sandwich and cup of treacle-thick espresso made her clamp her lips together for a second.

'Christmas breakfast of champions,' grinned Olive.

Ivy swallowed hard. Her mouth tasted like the wrong end of a badger.

'Trust me,' said Olive, looking a bit more sympathetic all of a sudden, 'you'll feel better for it.'

Ivy took a tentative sip of the coffee, followed by the tiniest nibble of the sandwich as wafts of warm bacon threatened to overwhelm her. Olive nodded approvingly and then disappeared back into the kitchen.

The moment she was on her own, Ivy stared around for the nearest toilet – just in case she needed to make a dash for it.

'Here,' said Olive, reappearing and plonking a pack of paracetamol on the bar next to Ivy's plate, along with a pint of water.

Ivy popped a couple of pills out of the pack and swallowed them with a careful sip of water.

Nectar of the gods!

She quickly took a much bigger mouthful, making Olive laugh.

'That's my girl,' she said, 'you'll be right as rain in twenty minutes.'

'What happened last night?' said Ivy, with a nervous glance over her shoulder. She needn't have worried – the pair of them were still alone.

'Well,' said Olive, 'you decided to take a special tour through my whiskey collection.'

'That explains a lot,' said Ivy.

'When you got to the fourth one, you started singing,' said Olive.

'I can't sing,' said Ivy.

'I'm the last person you need to tell that to,' said Olive. 'Then, when you got to number six - which is a very fine twelve-year-old malt by the way - you started dancing.'

'I don't really dance,' said Ivy weakly.

'I know!' laughed Olive. 'But it's alright, your secret's safe with me... and half of Crumcarey. But then you didn't dance for very long, so not *that* many people noticed... because you fell over pretty quickly.'

'I fell over?' said Ivy.

'Yep,' said Olive. 'I actually think you just fell asleep on your feet and toppled, because you were definitely snoring by the time you landed!'

Nice. Really classy Ivy!

'So... how come I didn't wake up down here on the floor this morning?' she said as a sense of doom settled over her. Here it came – the full, horrific truth.

'Connor carried you up to bed,' said Olive lightly, her eyes twinkling.

'No.' Ivy shook her head, her voice quite firm – as if

simple, flat-out denial could change what had happened.

'Oh yes,' said Olive, looking like she was thoroughly enjoying herself. 'And remind me when you come to settle your tab that I owe you a huge discount on your bill.'

'What for?' said Ivy faintly.

'For the floorshow!' she giggled. 'Honestly, you entertained the entire island!'

'Oh no. Oooooooh no!' groaned Ivy, covering her face with her hands.

'It's not that bad, love,' said Olive.

'But... I thought Connor was asleep?' she said through her fingers.

'He was... until you started singing!' said Olive. 'Apparently, you thought he was a *lovely man* and you told him right here in my bar.'

'I didn't?' groaned Ivy.

'You did! And then you asked him to marry you,' said Olive, pausing to wipe a tear from her eye.

'Not possible,' said Ivy, even though the wibbly, fuzzy memories of the previous evening were suddenly coming into focus.

'I've got plenty of witnesses if you don't believe me!' said Olive. 'Then I heard you asking him again on the way up the stairs. You told him you loved him. Then you said he had to put you down so that you could get down on one knee and – I quote – *"proposhe prop-lery"*. I didn't hear anything else after that because I was too busy laughing!'

Ivy slumped, face down on the bar, and covered her head with her arms.

Oh God, the shame of it.

'What happened then?' she mumbled.

'I have no idea,' said Olive. 'Connor never came back down, if that's what you're asking – and it was quite late by the time I went home.'

Oh. My. God.

Connor had carried her up the stairs to her room... and he'd not come back down again. Had she... *slept* with Connor?! This was *so* much worse than she'd ever imagined.

'Maybe he stayed in one of the other rooms,' said Olive with a shrug. 'He might still be around here somewhere.'

'You think?' said Ivy, a small bubble of hope forming in her chest.

'Not really,' said Olive, shaking her head.

The bubble promptly burst.

'His car's gone from outside,' she added. 'Looks like he made a break for it before you woke up!'

CHAPTER 13

'What am I going to do?' said Ivy, aware that her voice had risen in a kind of horrified whine.

'First – deep breaths!' said Olive looking decidedly amused. 'Come on now, follow me!'

Ivy copied Olive as she sucked in a huge, exaggerated lungful of air.

'And hooooold...' said Olive.

Ivy held her breath... and held her breath... she could feel her cheeks going red and let out a little squeak of discomfort.

'Okay – and release!' said Olive.

Ivy blew the breath out in a rush and gasped.

'See!' said Olive. 'Much better.'

'Erm... yeah - thanks... I think?' said Ivy, a smile forcing its way onto her face even though she was panting a bit.

'Well, it took your mind off things, didn't it?' demanded Olive with a wink.

'Yeah... No. Not really.'

'So, can you really not remember what happened last night?' asked Olive curiously.

Ivy shook her head. She still had fuzzy images of trying to kiss someone... and she could vaguely remember telling someone she loved them... and *maybe* a bit of dancing? But other than that, she was mostly drawing a blank. The problem was... in that blank, anything could have happened. Of course, she *had* woken up fully clothed... but that didn't *mean anything*, did it?

'Well, you're just going to have to ask Connor then, aren't you?' said Olive, as if it was the simplest solution in the world. 'He'll be here later for lunch – you can sort it all out then!'

Ivy's heart sank at the idea of talking to Connor in front of the entire population of Crumcarey as they sat down for their Christmas dinner. She stared at Olive in horror, but Olive had already turned back to her bowl of sprouts without a care in the world.

Slumping forwards, Ivy buried her face in her arms. This was the weirdest Christmas morning ever!

One thing bugging her more than all the rest - she simply wasn't the kind of girl to have a one-night stand... it wasn't her style. Especially the part where she got so drunk that she couldn't even remember

CHRISTMAS ON CRUMCAREY

whether it had actually happened or not. She was *definitely* not the kind of girl to cheat on someone.

Or was she?

She was certainly pretty angry with Gareth right now... and, after all, she already knew *that* relationship was as good as over. But *he* didn't, and that was the important part of the equation. That's what made this so much worse.

Sure, Gareth thought the way to move their relationship forward was by getting a dog... and *sure*, there was something about Connor that had made her just melt in a great big puddle of lust, but...

Ivy sighed. For a moment, the thought of Connor's strong arms wrapped around her as he carried her up the stairs made her lose her train of thought. Gareth had never so much as offered to give her a piggyback at a concert. There was no way he'd have been able to manoeuvre her up a full flight of stairs... at least not without breaking several bones in the process.

'You know,' said Ivy, raising her head, 'It's not just Connor I owe an apology to. I'm so sorry for my dreadful behaviour last night, Olive!'

'Ah, be off with you!' laughed Olive. 'Don't you worry about it! If you think that's the worst I've seen, you've got another thing coming. Of course, I can't speak for Connor. I don't know what you got up to upstairs!'

Ivy pulled a face. 'You know, there's no way I can wait until later to talk to him.'

'Well that problem's easy enough to fix,' said Olive. 'Why don't you just go over to his place?'

'On Christmas morning?' said Ivy, her eyes growing wide. 'I was thinking more along the lines of giving him a call - if you've got his number?'

'He hasn't got any signal up there,' muttered Olive, looking quickly down at her sprouts again. 'Anyway – this is Crumcarey – there's nothing strange about people appearing on your doorstep. Even on Christmas day!'

Ivy considered this for a couple of seconds. Compared to having the most awkward conversation of her life in front of a festive audience - she knew which option she preferred.

'How do I find his house?' said Ivy.

'It's a bit of a way,' said Olive.

'I could probably do with a walk!' said Ivy.

'Too far for that - you'll need some transport to get up there,' said Olive, shaking her head. 'Connor has a house on The Dot – that's our smallest island.'

'But... how'd I get over to him?' said Ivy, noticing that her hangover was just starting to pound right at the back of her eyeballs.

'There's a causeway that you can just walk over at low tide!' said Olive, glancing at her watch. 'If you go now, you should be there before the tide turns and covers it up again!'

Ivy blinked. She felt like she'd slipped sideways into some kind of alternate universe.

'But... but...' she stammered, 'I don't have a car.'

'Luckily, you're staying in just the right place!' said Olive. 'Follow me!'

Abandoning her bowl of sprouts on the bar, Olive beckoned for Ivy to follow her outside, pausing just long enough in the entrance for her to slip her trainers on and shrug into her mercifully dry coat.

'I can't believe it's not raining!' said Ivy, looking up at the blue sky as she followed Olive around the side of the Tallyaff. She wrapped her arms around her against the chilly breeze – but it was nothing compared to yesterday's howling gale.

The sun wasn't very high and didn't look like it was going to do much more than roll along the horizon before disappearing again around mid-afternoon. But still, it was a shock not to be drenched within seconds of leaving the shelter of the Tallyaff.

'It does happen sometimes, you know!' laughed Olive. 'The key thing to remember about the weather up here is - if you don't like it, you don't need to worry because it'll be doing something different in five minutes!'

'I'll try to remember that!' laughed Ivy. 'Erm, where are we going, by the way?' she asked curiously as Olive led her into a little yard at the back of the guesthouse.

'Well, among my many roles here on the island, I just happen to be the representative for the Crumcarey Car Hire company,' said Olive.

Of *course* she was!

Ivy grinned despite her hangover. Was there a single pie on Crumcarey Olive didn't have her finger in?

'We don't have a very large fleet of vehicles available - as you can imagine. We've only got one road, after all. But at least our vehicles are varied!'

Ivy stopped in her tracks. Olive could say that again.

Parked in the yard were two ancient estate cars and one huge tractor.

'Now, obviously, they appeal to all kinds of motorists visiting the island. The tractor is actually remarkably popular!' said Olive, putting on her best sales patter. 'Especially in the summer. People like the open air feel and its - you know - countryside charm.'

'I can't drive a tractor,' laughed Ivy, shaking her head and then promptly wishing she hadn't. The large whiskey-tinged ball bearings drummed from one side of her brain to the other.

'Well then,' said Olive drawing her towards the old, knackered estate cars, 'how about one of these instead?'

Ivy wrinkled her nose as she took a closer look through the window of the nearest one. It looked... pretty agricultural. In a way, more so than the tractor. The back was full of bits of straw and... other unmentionable... things. She turned to have a look at the other one, crossing her fingers that it might be in a slightly better state.

CHRISTMAS ON CRUMCAREY

Fat chance! If anything, the second car was even worse. This one was full of straw too... and poo. Plus this one had some strange scuffs inside and definitely what looked like some kind of hoof prints here and there.

'Now, I know what you're thinking,' said Olive, 'and I can get the back seats installed for you if you really want them.'

Ivy raised an eyebrow. She *really* hadn't given the lack of back seats any thought.

'But back seats would have to wait until tomorrow because I'm going to be a bit busy today cooking Christmas dinner... and although my lovely hubby is going to be here any moment, the poor lamb simply hasn't got the knack of it! It's a bit fiddly, you see.'

'Right...' said Ivy, wondering why she'd need the back seats anyway.

'Normally I'd ask Connor to fit them for you - but obviously, given that's who you're off to visit, that's not much help!'

'I think I can manage without!' said Ivy with a small smile. 'Front seats are all I need. So how much do these cost per day?'

'Hang on, let me think about this,' said Olive, closing her eyes and rubbing her chin. 'Now, Christmas is normally a really busy time, and that's when our premium rate applies. But I like you, Ivy, so we can put it on your tab, and I'll give you a discount!'

'As long as it's not for more singing,' sighed Ivy. 'The last lot's what got me in this trouble in the first place!'

'I won't make you sing for these,' said Olive with a smile. 'So, which one will it be?'

'Is there any difference?' said Ivy.

'You'd better believe it!' said Olive.

Ivy stared at them. They looked practically identical to her. They were the same model, make and colour. They both seemed to have roughly the same amount of scratches to the knackered navy paintwork. Neither one of them had a sunroof, but like Olive was now busy telling her, they'd be a complete waste of space on a damp island like Crumcarey.

'Okay – enlighten me!' said Ivy.

'Well, it's like this,' said Olive. 'Mr. Harris likes to drive his new-born calves around from field to field in this one, so it has a faint whiff of cow and... well, a cow's *you know what!*'

'Nice!' laughed Ivy, wrinkling her nose.

'The other one is favoured by Mrs McCluskey from down near Big Sandy. She's the wife of one of the fishermen. They're away on holiday at the moment.' Olive paused for a deep breath. 'Anyway, she uses it to transport her chickens around.'

'You're joking?' said Ivy.

'Deadly serious,' said Olive, 'and neither of them will ever use the other one's car.'

'So you're telling me that one of these is a cow taxi and the other one is a chicken bus?' said Ivy, her shoulders shaking with suppressed laughter.

'That's right,' said Olive, 'though if I'm being fair to Mrs McCluskey – she actually needs the car to deliver eggs.'

'So that one must smell better!' said Ivy.

'Well, no... not really... because Mrs McCluskey's chickens rather like being driven around the island,' said Olive. 'I think they like a bit of adventure... and you know what chickens are like.'

Ivy *didn't* really know what chickens were like... but she could say with her hand on her heart that she'd never met a flock of chickens who enjoyed being chauffeured around on day trips before.

'So... which one should I choose?' she said, feeling that she'd quite like to give up on the whole idea and go back to bed instead.

'It's hard to tell,' said Olive. 'I think it depends on which poo smell offends you more – cow or chicken? You know, this is the main reason the tractor is so popular. It's open to the elements. But then - you've already met the elements on Crumcarey, and they're no picnic either.'

'I'll go for the cow one,' said Ivy. The driver's seat looked a tiny little bit tidier... that was its only redeeming feature as far as she could see. 'Shall I do the paperwork when I get back?'

Olive threw her head back and laughed. 'Bless you, dearie. There isn't any paperwork. I mean, it's not like you can steal the car here. Where would you go? You're surrounded by the sea! And don't forget Mr Harris's sharks!'

Olive handed the key over, and Ivy dropped into the driver's seat, doing her best to breathe through her mouth as she closed the door.

'Actually,' said Ivy, quickly rolling down the window before Olive disappeared back inside the Tallyaff, 'I need some directions. I haven't got a clue how to get to The Dot!'

'Well,' said Olive, 'the good news is, it's practically impossible to get lost on Crumcarey. You either drive clockwise or anticlockwise... and that's pretty much it. Oh, and avoid the big blue wet bits!'

'Good advice!' laughed Ivy. 'And which direction should I choose?'

'I'd go for the clockwise route,' said Olive. 'That way you'll get to see Big Sandy - and you can maybe pick up an ice cream from my daughter's van. I know her and Frank were heading down there to the dunes this morning.'

'Are you serious?' said Ivy. 'On Christmas day?'

'Absolutely,' said Olive. 'It doesn't matter to those two lovebirds – they'll be out year-round. As long as they're together, I don't think they really care what day it is!'

'Aw!' sighed Ivy. 'Right... I'd better get this done!'

The stench inside the car was already making her eyes sting. She needed to get on the road to get some fresh air circulating.

'Go on - you head off,' laughed Olive, clearly noticing that she was struggling to keep her bacon sarnie in place again. 'And don't forget... if you need to puke - do your best not to do it into the wind!'

CHAPTER 14

*I*vy really hoped that her eyes would stop watering soon. After turning left onto the narrow "main road" from the Tallyaff, she'd wound the window down, opening it as wide open as she could get it. She might freeze on her way to Connor's – but it would be better than choking to death on the pungent whiff of Eau de Bovine. Maybe the chicken bus would have been a better choice after all. Sure, she hated feathers, but there was no way it could smell any worse than this!

Now that she was on her way, all Ivy had to do was distract herself from the rolling ball of nerves in her stomach. It felt incredibly rude to be turning up at a virtual stranger's house on Christmas morning smelling like a mixture of bag lady and cow poo. Of course, it didn't help that she was still wearing yesterday's clothes, but it wasn't like she could do much about that - she didn't have her case with her on the island after all. Still, she hated feeling quite so disgusting and grubby – especially when she'd be face to face with Connor again very soon.

If only she'd been able to grab a quick shower before heading out on this mad mission, but Olive had been adamant that there wasn't a second to waste - otherwise she'd be running the risk of the causeway disappearing as the tide came back in.

Ivy pulled in a deep breath in the hope that it might help her calm down - only to splutter in disgust at the stench. She quickly angled her face towards the open window, doing her best to get some slightly fresher air in her lungs. If only she was more familiar with the road, she'd be tempted to stick her head out of the window like a dog.

Frankly, the sooner she got to Connor's house, the better. Ivy knew she needed to apologise for her behaviour the previous evening... but even more than that, she needed to find out what had happened between them. But... she didn't want to let her head disappear down that rabbit hole right now, otherwise she'd be a blithering mess by the time she actually arrived. Instead, she turned her attention very determinedly to the scenery as it unfolded around her.

It soon became very clear that there really was no need to worry about getting lost on Crumcarey. Just as Olive had said, there was just one road with little offshoots towards cottages and farms here and there.

She'd left the airport and the harbour behind her ages ago and was now trundling through gorgeous countryside.

Actually – *through* was the wrong word. The countryside was to her right-hand side, and to her left sat the jagged coastal cliffs which dipped away here and there to reveal a sudden beach or hidden cove. Beyond that – sea the kind of blue that only belonged in kid's books. The tide might be out at the moment, but the rolling turquoise waves took her breath away.

There was no mistaking Big Sandy when she came to it – it more than lived up to its name. Golden-white sand stretched away along a sweeping curve almost as far as the eye could see.

Ivy slowed right down, trying to take it all in, not that she'd dare drive particularly fast on this narrow coastal road anyway. That said, the road was in surprisingly good condition – and she hadn't spotted another car at all so far. There was also the issue that the cow taxi seemed to be stuck in second gear and wouldn't budge no matter how hard she tried. All that happened were some horrific grinding sounds that did nothing to soothe Ivy's already tender head.

So, Ivy continued to crawl along, admiring the view as the fresh island air pouring in through the window began to work its magic on her hangover. If it wasn't for the constant stench of cow, it would actually be quite pleasant.

She couldn't believe the difference in the weather

compared to the day before - where she'd been soaked the moment she'd stepped outside and almost blown off her feet more than once. This morning, the sky was a perfect blue – though there were piles of dramatic clouds far out to sea. Ivy wondered if they'd get another storm before the day was out.

The wind was still very much in effect, though Ivy had a feeling that it was pretty much a permanent feature here in Crumcarey. She could feel it buffeting the car as if it was trying to sweep her right off the road. At least it was hitting the passenger side, so she wasn't getting it full force in the face!

This place really was an undiscovered beauty spot. The road headed down a gentle slope so that she was soon driving level with the dunes that skirted Big Sandy. Ivy admired the mounds of crystal sand and tussocky, windswept grass, marvelling at the fact there wasn't a single soul in sight.

Just as the thought crossed her mind, Ivy spotted something ahead that stuck out like a sore thumb... and proved her wrong. A jaunty pink, custard and cream ice cream van was tucked into the dunes, clearly angled so that it was as sheltered as possible from the blasting wind.

This must be Olive's daughter's van! Ivy had half-thought that Olive was joking about them being open today - but there it was, right in front of her. Even going as slowly as she was, Ivy shot past the van before she really believed it was there at all. She was pretty sure she'd spotted someone staring out through the little hatch at her though!

For a moment, Ivy considered finding somewhere to turn around so that she could go back to say hello and treat herself to an ice cream. Then she quickly decided that might be an even worse plan than turning up on Connor's doorstep on Christmas morning. There was no way that her stomach would be able to handle rich, creamy mint choc chip just yet. The whiskey needed a little while longer to leave her system. Besides, the idea of eating anything in this car felt decidedly unhygienic!

As she trundled on, with the never-ending stretch of Big Sandy to her left, Ivy couldn't help the huge smile that crept up and plastered itself across her face. She'd never been on an adventure like this... and even though she was heading towards what was likely to be the most excruciating conversation of her entire life... she was secretly loving every second of it!

As Ivy rounded a curve in the road that led uphill and away from the beach, she spotted the stench-culprits themselves. There, in front of her, were some very well-groomed cows. They were all gathered around a spot of fence that looked like it had been newly lashed together with a piece of rope.

The lumbering animals didn't seem at all worried by the vicious wind as it ruffled their fluffy fur, making them look a bit like they were auditioning for a shampoo advert. Ivy slowed down even further to have a good look as she drove past, and the hairy coos stared straight back, munching away without a care in the world.

As she left the cows behind her, Ivy reached to turn the radio on only for her hand to grapple with empty space. It wasn't so much that the radio didn't work... it simply wasn't there. She glanced down quickly, only to be faced with a mess of wires and connectors. Damn! She'd been rather hoping for a bit of a Christmas singsong as a kind of festive middle finger to Gareth.

Oh well -she'd just have to do without accompaniment. Ivy started to hum Good King Wenceslas. She really couldn't sing for toffee... but who cared? It was only her in the car, so it didn't really matter.

At least... it didn't matter until it reminded her of the night before. She must have made such an epic prat out of herself. She gave a little squirm of embarrassment which promptly turned into nerves as she remembered exactly why she was out on this magical mystery tour on Christmas morning in the first place.

'I'm not sure this is a good ideaaaaaaaa!' she sang, starting to chuckle to herself. She needed to watch she didn't crack the windows with that kind of pitch! Still - Ivy held with the sentiment. She was about to turn up on Connor's doorstep on Christmas morning to ask if she'd slept with him whilst practically pickled on whiskey. If someone did that to her, she'd have thought they were completely stone barking mad. But then, maybe she was.

Ramping up her volume even further, Ivy promptly switched over to jingle bells. She was only two lines in when, out of nowhere, it started to rain.

Okay – she knew her singing was bad, but really?!

The rain promptly turned to sleet, then switched to hail which bounced off the car and all over the road... but by the time Ivy found the windscreen wiper, it stopped as if someone had flipped a switch and the sun had come out again.

'Officially. Insane. Island!' she muttered, as the car chugged its way up another gentle incline.

As soon as she crested the brow, Ivy realised that she was nearing her destination. A little way ahead, she spotted The Dot. Currently, with the tide out, she could also see the old stone causeway that linked the tiny island with this one. It wasn't far out at all – but far enough that she wouldn't want to attempt the swim when the tide came back in!

When Olive had been describing it to Ivy, she'd probably been a bit over-generous... The Dot was truly tiny - a grass-topped mound of rock perched out in the sea. As she drove closer, Ivy realised that there was only one house on the island... but *oh* what a house!

'Oh my goodness,' Ivy said to herself, staring at the fairy-tale cottage. It was absolutely stunning.

If only she was heading there to spend a cosy Christmas with friends rather than rocking up as the most awkward, unexpected guest this island had ever witnessed. Ah well – it was time to face the music!

Ivy pulled the car onto a grassy spot off the road that overlooked the causeway. There was already another car there – Ivy guessed it was probably Connor's. So – he was home then. She quickly reminded herself that most normal people *were* home at this time on Christmas morning!

Holding her breath, Ivy wound up the window. Then, gripping the door tightly in case of any rogue gusts of wind, she climbed out quickly. She had to throw her entire body weight against the door as she battled with the wind to get it to closed.

'Wow!' she gasped, finally managing to close the car door. It lulled you into a bit of a false sense of security when you were inside the car. The weather might *look* friendlier today – but it was clearly a cunning ruse to trick unwary visitors!

Even so, it felt amazing to be out of the stinking car. Ivy could feel the cool, salty air on her face as she headed down the grassy bank onto the sand and then hopped up onto the causeway.

Her feet instantly slid a little on a green, slimy patch of weed. Ivy flung her arms out wide to help her keep her balance and took a couple of steps. Right – as long as she avoided the green patches, the rest of it felt fairly safe. She'd head straight along the middle – just in case of any extra-strong blasts of wind.

Even though the hailstorm had been fleeting, it had dusted the ragged lawn around Connor's cottage with crystals that gleamed in the low, wintry sunlight. Ivy guessed that it would probably disappear in just a couple of minutes, but right now it made The Dot look magical.

Frankly, she had a feeling that Connor's house probably looked like an oil painting whatever the weather was doing. The old-fashioned white cottage with its heavy slate roof and thick walls was possibly the cosiest and most inviting place Ivy had ever seen.

What an amazing place to live! Ivy couldn't help but compare it to her tiny flat. Hardly a dream home at the best of times, and about a thousand times worse because Gareth lived there! What had she been thinking?

Ivy paused for a moment and peered over the edge of the causeway down into the crystal waters lapping at the sides. If what Olive had told her was true, this pathway would disappear under the water before long. Then, she guessed Connor's beautiful cottage would be cut off from reality until the next low tide.

A little shiver ran down Ivy's spine and she wrapped her arms around herself. Getting stuck on a tiny island with Gareth would have been like a waking nightmare, but getting stuck here with Connor? Well... that would be something else entirely.

What if something magical was actually happening here? Maybe the faulty plane and the ferry being out of action had happened just to lead her towards Connor! His beautiful cottage was just the icing on the cake - snow pun not intended, of course! What if meeting Connor was what this Christmas was all about?!

Ivy gave a little wriggle of excitement. Any minute now, she'd see him again and it would all be clear. She took a couple of excited steps towards The Dot and then stopped again. What if she smelled of cow poo? It was almost guaranteed by this point, wasn't it? She'd been in the car for maybe, what, ten minutes? She was bound to have picked up at least a light whiff of farmyard.

Ivy lifted an arm and tried to give herself a quick sniff test. She couldn't smell anything, but then her nose was still burning from the journey over here, and the wind was making her nose and eyes run, so it would be kind of hard to tell.

Oh well, there was no way she was about to turn back now. She tried to reassure herself that Connor would understand – after all, he probably knew all about the cow car anyway, didn't he? He'd probably already spotted it as the cottage windows looked right down across the causeway and towards Crumcarey.

Anyway – now that she'd come this far, Ivy wanted a closer look at his stunning cottage. It was almost too perfect for words and it made the little cottage she'd hoped she'd be staying in with Gareth look like a ruin in comparison! It looked so inviting with golden light spilling from the little windows, wood smoke curling from one of the chimneys, and a bright, cheerful wreath of driftwood and berries on the front door.

Ivy stepped down from the causeway and made her way towards the cottage. This really was the smallest speck of land she could ever imagine someone living on. She barely needed to turn her hand to see it in its entirety.

The only thing the cottage seemed to be missing was a garden - but then, Ivy guessed that any pots and plants would probably be blown away the minute you turned your back. Perhaps there was room for a little conservatory or something on the other side, out of the wind...

Ivy blushed as she caught herself already making plans for what she would do with the place if she moved in. Maybe she was taking her festive fantasy a little bit too far... she didn't know if Connor was even talking to her after what had happened last night.

Ivy came back to reality with a bump.

What *had* happened last night? Urgh... the real reason for her visit slapped her around the face like a week-old slice of turkey.

Well – she was here now. It was time to ask some questions, make her apologies... and possibly skedaddle back across that causeway as fast as her hungover little legs could carry her.

Doing her best to make herself look at least slightly presentable, Ivy ran her fingers through her hair before realising it was totally pointless as the wind whipped it around her in a mad halo. Sod it. It was time. Taking one last deep breath, Ivy knocked firmly on Connor's front door.

Nothing.

Not a single sound.

Ivy started counting under her breath. She'd give it until ten, and then she'd leave.

She'd just reached eight when the door creaked open.

'Connor – I'm so sorry to turn up on your doorstep like this, but after last night I wanted to say...' she ground to a halt.

It wasn't Connor facing her, but a young, ridiculously beautiful woman.

'You were saying?' she said, raising an eyebrow.

CHAPTER 15

❄

Ivy stood there, her mouth hanging open stupidly as she stared at the woman in front of her. Her addled brain was feverishly trying to come up with an excuse as to why she was here... anything other than the truth, of course! How did you tell someone that you were there to ruin their Christmas day? Heck, how could she tell this beautiful woman that she may or may not have had a drunken one-night stand with her boyfriend... or husband... or whatever.

Happy Christmas, I'm here to ruin your life!

With everything Olive had gossiped to her about, how could she have conveniently forgotten to mention that Connor lived here with his other half? His stunningly beautiful other half who was currently making Ivy feel almost as bad as she probably smelled!

One thing was now certain – whatever had happened last night had been a terrible, terrible mistake. So was coming here. How on earth was she going to get out of it now? She couldn't exactly pretend that she'd called at the wrong house by mistake, could she? There was only one house on the whole bloody island. What a mess!

Ivy turned and glanced nervously behind her. Maybe there was a tree she could hide behind or something? But of course, just like over on Crumcarey, there wasn't a single tree here on The Dot! Maybe she should just make a dash for it and sprint back over the causeway... but in her hungover state, she'd probably just end up toppling into the sea.

Like a total idiot, Ivy realised that her knees had just started to shake. She needed to man up. She turned back to face the woman only to find her grinning in amusement.

'You must be Ivy,' she giggled.

Ivy nodded dumbly.

'You know, my brother told me all about you. According to him, you have a lovely singing voice!'

Ivy felt like a great big wave had just swept down the causeway and crashed right over her head. Her face was tingling in shocked relief as the word "brother" bounced around her skull.

'Your brother?' she echoed – sounding almost drunk with hope.

The woman nodded, her long dark hair dancing around her face.

'Yes. Connor - my brother. He's been talking about you non-stop since he got back.'

'He has?' said Ivy in a daze, watching as the woman brought a slender hand up to push her hair back in a gleaming sheet.

The woman nodded, smirking. 'Yep – that's my big brother. Total idiot. Oh, I'm Rowan by the way! You know, you'd better come in. Connor's just jumped in the shower. He'll be out in a minute.'

'Maybe I should go,' said Ivy. She was still in a total daze. What was she even thinking, turning up here on Christmas morning? And what was she going to say to Connor anyway? *"Oh hi – I just wanted to double check with you – did we shag last night...? Because I was way too drunk to remember!"*

'You can't go!' said Rowan, grabbing Ivy's hand and tugging her inside the cottage, closing the door firmly behind her. 'He'll never forgive me if I let you go before he gets to see you.'

Ivy raised her eyebrows. Uh oh... was she in for a piece of his mind? Maybe she had more to apologise for than just her awful singing. If only she could remember!

'I promise you he won't be very long,' said Rowan, a cheeky smile still on her face. 'That's a definite because I used all the hot water earlier! But frankly, it serves him right for abandoning me on Christmas Eve, and then stopping off to help Mr Harris with his cows on his way home.'

Ivy remembered passing the well-groomed, fluffy cows, all staring intently at what looked like a newly patched bit of fence.

'What happened with the cows?' she asked. Well, it was something to say, wasn't it? And at least it kept them off the topic of Connor for a few seconds.

'Oh, they'd decided to go for a bit of a wander apparently. Happens quite a lot,' said Rowan with a shrug as she led Ivy along the hall. 'Connor just ushered them back in and found a bit of old rope to sort out the fence until he can head over later and help Mr Harris mend it properly.'

Ivy nodded vaguely, staring around her with interest. The cottage was very different to what she'd been expecting. Outside, it had been the perfect chocolate-box picture, but inside it was a different story. Clearly, it would *eventually* be the cosy cottage she'd been daydreaming about on her way over here, but right now, it was more of a building site than anything else.

'Come on through to the sitting room!' said Rowan. 'Well... perhaps sitting room is a bit misleading given there's nowhere to actually sit but...' she trailed off.

Ivy followed Rowan into a room that would be absolutely gorgeous when it was finished, with its window overlooking the causeway and facing Crumcarey over the stretch of water. But right now – it didn't have any furniture... or carpet... or very much else either.

To be fair to Connor though, there were Christmas decorations everywhere. There was a stepladder lined with tinsel, and the cordless power tools that seemed to be lying on every available surface were all wearing little paper hats.

The one bit of comfort the room did have going for it was a cute wood burner with a stack of driftwood next to it. The fire was pumping out enough heat to make Ivy break into a sweat almost instantly. Oh no, that was just going to enliven the smell of cow, wasn't it?

Ivy clamped her arms firmly to her sides and made a mental note to stay as still as possible to limit any possible offensive wafts.

'You look a bit warm,' said Rowan cheerfully. 'Why don't you take your coat off?'

Ivy quickly shook her head. 'You're okay... I'm fine!' she said with a squeak, wiping a bead of sweat off her brow.

'You know, I did tell Connor this fire was too big for the room, but did he listen to me? Joys of being a little sister, eh?!' she chuckled. 'Big brother always knows best!'

Ivy smiled, not really knowing what to say... or what to do with herself. It didn't seem to matter though, as Rowan was in full flow.

'Anyway, Connor said he got offered the wood

burner for free – so he grabbed it! It would have only ended up going rusty outside someone's house otherwise. It's a bit like that here on Crumcarey – probably the same on any small island community, I should imagine. Share and share alike and all that jazz!'

Ivy's eyes widened.

'*Not* like that!' snorted Rowan. 'I can see you and I are going to get along! Anyway - do you want something to drink?'

Ivy, who was starting to feel like a bit of a lemon just standing there as there was nothing to sit down on... or even perch against... nodded gratefully.

'There's tea, but there isn't any coffee I'm afraid. Connor took his entire stash down to the boatshed and drank the whole bloody lot!' Rowan rolled her eyes. 'He's promised to stay off it for a bit... I think he gave himself the caffeine jitters trying to get that engine sorted!'

'Tea would be really nice, thanks,' said Ivy.

'Cool. Make yourself at home... as much as you can! Sorry there isn't really anywhere to sit at the moment. Apparently, Connor's waiting on Terry Livingston to get back from his holiday because he's supposed to be throwing out his old sofa.' Rowan smirked at Ivy conspiratorially. 'I don't know why Conor doesn't just get a new one. I mean, he captains the ferry so it wouldn't cost him anything to bring over... but then, that's my brother for you. I think you get a bit like that when you've lived on such a tiny island for so long.'

CHRISTMAS ON CRUMCAREY

The smell of fresh, lemony soap made Ivy freeze. Was that...?

'Get like what, exactly?'

Connor's voice rumbled from behind her and Ivy felt herself break into a sweat all over again. She turned her head slowly, only to find him leaning lazily against the unpainted doorframe. He looked practically edible.

'Get like a tight-arse!' said Rowan, wandering over and poking him in the stomach. 'Oh – by the way, Ivy's here to see you!'

'I thought I heard voices... but then I thought it was just you playing with your imaginary friends, Row!' said Connor, ruffling his sister's hair.

'Haha, you're so funny – I don't think!' sighed Rowan. 'Anyway, if you get out of my way so I can go and make Ivy some tea.'

Connor shuffled into the room, letting Rowan pass him, and then he turned to smile at Ivy, who promptly felt her knees go all funny.

'Tea for me too!' Connor yelled, making Ivy jump.

'Yes, I know!' came Rowan's huff from halfway down the hall.

'Hi!' said Connor, in a lower voice. 'Erm... Merry Christmas.'

'You too,' said Ivy, her voice coming out all tight and scratchy.

Man, she was nervous!

'I thought I might be seeing you again,' said Connor.

'But I thought maybe later - at the Tallyaff for Christmas dinner.'

'About last night…'

Ivy winced. Okay – so that had come out blunt and loud – not a particularly winning combination, but there wasn't any point beating around the bush, was there? She may as well tell him the reason she was here, and it was probably best to have this conversation while Rowan was out of earshot.

'Yeah,' said Connor, scuffing his toe into the bare concrete floor. 'About last night. We slept together.'

Oh. My. God!

How could he have just blurted it out like that? What a heartless…!

'It's not what you're thinking,' said Connor quickly, holding his hands up like he was begging her not to shoot.

'How? What?' Ivy rubbed her eyes. She was never drinking whiskey again. Especially the lethal twelve-year-old kind. 'Explain!' she finally gasped.

'We didn't *sleep* sleep together,' said Connor, running his fingers through his damp hair. 'Not in *that* way. I mean… we slept in the same bed, but… you were under three duvets and I was just under the blanket on top.'

What was it with this family? The pair of them had both attempted to give her a heart attack in the space of ten minutes!

Ivy blew out a long, low breath as she glared at

Connor, holding his eye for a long second as she tried to figure out if he was telling the truth. But then... why would he lie?

Feeling a blush start to spread across her hot cheeks, Ivy dropped her eyes to the concrete floor. She felt strange. A huge wave of relief was coursing through her body, making her feel practically lightheaded – but there was something else mixed in there too... something that felt strangely like disappointment.

CHAPTER 16

❄

Ivy sank, cross-legged, onto the concrete floor. Her knees had had enough of trying to hold her up – and she finally just gave in.

This was officially the weirdest Christmas morning she'd ever had. Where were the tartan pyjamas? Where was the pile of Christmas presents and the glittering tree? Instead of all that, here she was on a concrete floor surrounded by a bunch of power tools wearing paper Christmas hats. Standing in front of her, looking more than a little bit concerned, was the most beautiful man she'd ever seen.

'I really did mean to stay and explain,' said Connor. 'I know I should have... but you were completely zonked and I had no idea if I should wake you up... and I had to get back to the house because I felt bad for leaving Rowan on her own for so long. I mean – she comes to stay with me and I abandon her on Christmas morning!'

Ivy glanced over towards the door. Rowan had yet to make a reappearance and Ivy had the sneaking suspicion that she might be out in the hallway, laughing her head off as she listened to every word Connor was saying.

'And last night - I only closed my eyes for a second,' Connor ploughed on. 'I'm so sorry. I didn't mean for it to happen. I was just exhausted - you saw how knackered I was. Hell, I was fast asleep on the bar… or I was until you started singing.'

'Sorry,' said Ivy, finally getting a word in edgeways – but Connor didn't seem to hear.

'I think carrying you up to your room used up the last bit of energy I had left on emergency reserve. And then you kept slurring all those stupid, lovely things in my ear even though you'd only just met me…'

Ivy dropped her eyes and stared hard at the concrete floor again.

Could this get any more embarrassing?!

'…and then I was a bit worried that you might be sick in the night…'

That answered that question, then!

'Anyway, I thought I'd better stay and watch you. I only meant to stay for a little bit – but then I made the mistake of closing my eyes.'

Ivy nodded and opened her mouth to tell him that it was fine… that she understood… but he just carried on.

. . .

'Anyway, that's how it happened. The next thing I knew, it was the morning. I know I should have left a note or something, but there wasn't a pen or paper. And it's not like it was something I could explain on a bit of paper anyway... and...'

Ivy couldn't help herself - she started to giggle. Connor stared at her as if she'd just grown a second head.

'S-s-sorry!' gasped Ivy, trying to catch her breath. 'Just... your f-f-face!'

Ivy's whole body was shaking with laughter now. Poor old Connor was so busy tying himself up in knots and apologising for what had happened. But it was obvious to Ivy now that nothing had happened at all, other than one very tired person and one *very* drunk person falling asleep next to each other! Everything Connor had done last night was completely innocent and rather sweet.

As much as Ivy would *love* to think she could entice this gorgeous man she could barely keep her eyes off, she wasn't about to fool herself. He was clearly way out of her league. Besides, even if by some miracle she could, last night was definitely not the way she'd want it to happen. Especially not while she was technically still involved with someone else!

'I'm really sorry you ended up stuck here for Christmas,' said Connor. 'I did everything I could to get the engine back in the ferry, but it just couldn't be done in time. I did think about rowing you across to the mainland, but that would have been dangerous and stupid. It was dark and I was exhausted and...'

Connor stopped again. It looked like he'd finally noticed that Ivy was smiling at him.

'And I guess I'm sorry for your fiancé too,' he muttered as an afterthought.

'Liar...'

Ivy turned her head to see a grinning Rowan standing in the doorway, bearing a tray with three mugs of tea at a pack of biscuits.

'Shut it sis!' growled Connor. 'Anyway Ivy - are we okay?' he added.

Ivy grinned at him and nodded. 'We're fine. Besides, it's me who should be apologising to you.'

'What for?' said Connor.

'Waking you up with my terrible singing, for one thing,' said Ivy.

'He told me it was really good,' said Rowan, wandering over and setting the tray on the floor before sinking down next to Ivy.

Ivy pulled a face and Connor snorted.

'I promise you, I can't sing a note!' said Ivy, gratefully accepting a mug of tea and wrapping her fingers around it as she watched Connor wander towards the window.

He ran his fingers distractedly through his damp

hair and stared out at the causeway, and then turned to Ivy with a look of horror.

'Don't tell me you came all this way in the cow car?' he said.

Ivy nodded.

'Interesting choice!' laughed Connor. 'I think I would have picked the tractor.'

'Me too,' said Rowan around a mouthful of Rich Tea biscuit.

'But... I can't drive a tractor,' said Ivy, suddenly feeling like she'd missed out on something important as a kid. 'Besides, on my way over here it rained, sleeted and then hailed!'

'That's a quiet weather day on Crumcarey!' said Connor.

'That was all in the space of about twenty seconds!' said Ivy.

'You'll get used to it,' said Connor.

Something warm blossomed in Ivy's chest. The idea of staying on the island long enough to get used to the bonkers weather felt strangely wonderful.

No, no, no, no, no! This wasn't the plan at all! This was just a strange little Christmas interlude. Sure, it would make a great story when she got home, but that was it. Nothing life changing.

Ivy sighed. *Home.* Somehow, that word didn't hold much in the way of comfort anymore. She was dreading getting back to her tiny little flat. It had always been a bit of a refuge before she'd got together with Gareth, but ever since he'd moved in, it just hadn't been the same.

'So,' said Rowan, interrupting her spiralling thoughts, 'what does your fiancé think about you being stuck here with my brother for Christmas?'

Uh oh! There it was again... that dreaded word *fiancé!* She'd known the moment she'd first said it that it would cause her some kind of grief... well, it looked like her "little white lie" was back to bite her on the bottom, didn't it?!

It had seemed like a good ruse at the time, when she'd been desperate to get off the island. She couldn't believe that had been just yesterday!

'I can't imagine he's too pleased to be back on the mainland alone for Christmas while you're drinking tea in another man's house!' Rowan continued.

'Row!' hissed Connor. 'Seriously!'

Rowan turned to eyeball Ivy. 'I'm so sorry!' she said, looking horrified and leaning forward to grab Ivy's hand. 'I'm only teasing!'

Ivy forced a smile onto her face, shook her head and then gently retrieved her hand. As far as she could tell, she had two choices. She could either keep the fib going and dig herself an even deeper hole than the one she was already in, or she could come clean about everything – no matter how embarrassing it was going to be.

'Erm...' said Ivy, 'there's something I need to tell you. It's like this. I'm not *actually* engaged.'

Then she told them everything. About Gareth, and the motel, and the dog, and the flight over here. Ivy got a bit choked up when she told them that she was planning to end things with Gareth the minute she was back on the mainland with him.

'Oh you poor lamb, don't be upset!' said Rowan, patting her on the shoulder.

Ivy shook her head quickly and let out an embarrassed snort of laughter. 'I hate to admit this – but these are tears of relief!'

She glanced over at Connor, and he smiled back at her. 'What I don't get is how you ended up over here on your own!' he said.

'Gareth got in a mood and decided not to come with me,' she sighed, only just stopping herself from adding a fervent *"thank God"* at the end.

'Well, that's his loss,' said Connor, looking decidedly cheerful for some reason.

'Yes,' sighed Ivy. 'Crumcarey is an amazing place.

'I'm not talking about Crumcarey,' said Connor.

Ivy returned his smile shyly, her heart hammering.

'Witter-wooooo!' chuckled Rowan, who was clearly intent on wreaking havoc. She started making kissing sounds, waving her fingers around in the air in a heart shape.

'Hey!' growled Connor, 'quit it!'

'Make me!' said Rowan, pulling a face at him.

Connor promptly grabbed a dustcover that was sitting in a heap on the floor and flung it over his sister's head, before sinking down to sit next to her.

Ivy grinned as Rowan re-emerged and tried to grab Connor in a headlock. Somehow, watching the pair of them play-fighting was the most Christmassy thing that had happened all day.

'You okay now, Ivy?' panted Rowan once the pair of them had called a truce.

'Yeah, thanks!' said Ivy, letting out a sigh. 'Now all I've got to do is get over the fact that wasted almost two years of my life with him. I'm such an idiot!'

'Yeah - been there!' said both Connor and Rowan in unison.

Ivy raised her eyebrows. 'Give over!'

'You don't get to claim all the glory,' said Connor.

'Yeah, you definitely don't,' said Rowan. 'We'd be here until New Year if I listed all the stupid things I've done in my relationships.'

'I'll second that!' said Connor. 'And the worst part about it is, you just don't see it at the time, do you?'

'At least you don't bump into your exes all the time,' said Rowan. 'You just put them on the first plane off the island and wave goodbye. Or if it's been really bad, you've got the option of pushing them off the ferry.'

Connor snorted. 'I've not resorted to that one yet – but thanks for the idea!'

'But I'm right though, aren't I?' persisted Rowan. 'That's it for you – once they're gone, you don't have to see them again. They can either choose to come back to Crumcarey, knowing for sure that they'll bump into you...'

'That's never happened!' said Connor.

'Precisely,' sighed Rowan.

'Where do you live?' asked Ivy with interest.

'Edinburgh,' said Rowan.

'Well... surely you don't bump into your exes all the time, either?' said Ivy.

'You'd be surprised,' said Rowan. 'That place is more like living in a village – everyone knows everyone.'

'Yeah,' laughed Connor, 'poor old Rowan is running out of options... she's going to have to move soon – she's dated the entire city!'

'Oi!' squealed Rowan, thumping Connor on the arm.

'Okay, okay, maybe time to change the subject!' chuckled Connor as he got to his feet, gathering their mugs together. 'I'll teach you to drive a tractor if you'd like, Ivy?'

'Say no – say no!' giggled Rowan. 'I'll do it! Big brother here is much better in boats. Put him in a tractor and he's all over the place... and you've seen the width of the roads around here.'

'Right, that's it!' said Connor, grabbing the dust sheet and dropping it over her head again.

CHAPTER 17

❄

The three of them had had so much fun chatting and laughing, they completely lost track of time. As Connor gathered together their discarded cups from yet another round of tea, he happened to glance out of the window.

'Shit - the tide!' he gasped.

Ivy and Rowan both scrambled up and joined him.

'Blimey, that was quick!' said Ivy, watching the small waves that were already lapping up and over their only route back to Crumcarey.

'It's okay, we haven't left it too late,' said Rowan. 'But if we don't leave in a minute, we're going to get cut off.'

Ivy shrugged. She didn't mind the idea of getting cut off here with these two until the tide went back out again.

'Don't give him that look!' said Rowan, noticing

Ivy's sly glance towards Connor. 'We'd end up eating each other for Christmas dinner – this man has absolutely no food in the house!'

'I normally do,' said Connor, sounding defensive. 'It's just because I've been at the ferry terminal the entire time – and I knew we were eating at the Tallyaff today. You know what it's like after one of Olive's meals – you basically don't need to eat for a week afterwards!'

'I'll give you that point,' said Rowan, nodding her agreement and rubbing her stomach as if in anticipation of a piled plate.

'So... what do you normally do when The Dot gets cut off?' asked Ivy curiously. 'You can't just get stuck over here for hours at a time, can you?'

'Nah,' said Connor, shaking his head. 'I've got a little boat I usually keep moored just down by the edge of the causeway, but I took it over to the ferry terminal a few days ago to give it a sand and lick of paint.'

'Great timing,' said Rowan, rolling her eyes.

'It gets all the jobs done at the same time,' said Connor. 'Usually, everything's pretty quiet over Christmas. Obviously, I wasn't expecting special guests!'

'He definitely means you, not me!' huffed Rowan.

Ivy smiled at Connor and gave him a playful nudge with her elbow. Even as she did it, she couldn't help but think how weird it was that she felt so comfortable around this guy. Jeez – they'd only met for the first time just yesterday!

Connor locked eyes with her and returned her smile.

'Yeah, so… I hate to interrupt the pair of you while you're being so sickeningly cute,' said Rowan, 'but we definitely need to get a wiggle on. Otherwise, Christmas lunch is going to be a shared tin of beans - and that's best case scenario.'

'I've got water from the tap,' said Connor.

'Yeah, great. Thanks, big bro,' laughed Rowan, 'but that's definitely not the hospitality I'm expecting.'

'Okay – you've got a point,' said Connor. 'Come on, let's grab our stuff. Be right back, Ivy!'

Ivy watched, slightly dazed, as the pair of them dashed from the room, elbowing each other out of the way in an attempt to be first up the stairs. Two seconds later, she could hear them thundering around above her head as they gathered their things.

Letting out a huge sigh, Ivy stared around the half-finished room. She'd actually be sorry to leave The Dot. This morning had promised to be a total disaster, but it had turned out to be rather wonderful so far. She wondered if she'd ever come back here… or see the house when it was finished. Ivy swallowed hard as a little spike of sadness went through her. Of course she wouldn't! She'd be back on the mainland in a day or two… back to real life and all the disappointment that entailed.

※

Five minutes later, the three of them were lined up outside, staring out across the causeway towards Crumcarey. The path was already several inches deep in sloshing seawater.

Ivy wasn't much looking forward to this – she remembered how slippery it was in places – and that was before it was underwater! She glanced down at her feet and pulled a face. The other two were both wearing wellington boots, but all she had was her tatty pair of trainers – she was going to get soaked!

'Come on, Ivy. Hop on,' said Connor.

Ivy looked at him in surprise. 'Excuse me?'

'Piggyback time! Looks like I get to carry you again,' said Connor.

'It's becoming a bit of a habit with you two,' said Rowan, waggling her eyebrows at Ivy.

Doing her best to ignore Rowan's twinkling eyes, Ivy stared at Connor with her heart pounding. Now that she wasn't blind drunk, the idea of wrapping her legs around this man and letting him trudge her over the causeway felt more than a little bit intimidating.

Still, he had a big cheeky grin on his face and clearly wasn't going to take no for an answer.

Fine. If that's what it was going to take to keep her feet dry, then Merry Christmas Ivy!

'Come on!' laughed Connor. 'At least I know what I'm in for this time… and the longer we leave it, the more difficult this is going to get!'

'He's speaking from experience,' chuckled Rowan, taking the lead and sloshing ahead.

Without hesitating any longer, Ivy clambered up onto Connor's back. It was actually a bit of a relief. The wind was getting stronger again, but as she snuggled against Connor's back, she revelled in the shelter and the lemony waves of warmth.

The chilly breeze was now turning the rips of the rippling waves heading over the causeway into frothy foam, but Ivy felt completely safe. She wasn't even slightly worried that Connor might drop her. She wrapped her arms around his shoulders and held on as tightly as she could - not because she thought she was going to slip or anything, but because… why not? When would she ever have such a perfect excuse to hug this amazing man so tightly?

Sadly, they reached the safety of the shores of Crumcarey far too soon for Ivy's liking. She didn't really want the moment to be over.

'You can let go now,' said Connor.

Oops – busted!

Connor had clearly noticed that she was more than happy perching on his back. Ivy feel the blush spreading over her face as slid down. It was only as she caught sight of the cow taxi that she was reminded how awful she probably smelled… and she'd just been wrapped around Connor…

Awkward!

Ah well, it was too late to worry about that now.

Though, the minute they reached the Tallyaff, she was going straight upstairs for a much-needed bath!

Ivy stumbled slightly as a rogue gust of wind caught her off guard. Connor's hand was quickly on her shoulder, holding her steady.

'Okay?' he asked.

'Thanks,' muttered Ivy, nodding. She suddenly felt ridiculously shy of this lovely guy. She'd felt so comfortable around him all morning, too! Maybe The Dot really did have some kind of magic to it, and now that they were over on Crumcarey again, the spell was wearing off.

Ivy smiled at him again and then turned to head towards the cow taxi. 'I'll see you guys there?' she said over her shoulder.

'Oh no you don't! laughed Connor. 'There's no way I'm letting you drive all the way back to the Tallyaff in that thing.'

'Yeah,' said Rowan 'I agree with Connor. I want to show you some of the island on the way back, but there's no way I'm catching a lift with you in that thing - I don't want to end up smelling like cow all day!'

'Oh, God,' said Ivy with a shudder, 'I was kind of hoping you hadn't noticed that!'

Rowan let out a snort. 'Sorry lovely, but it's kind of hard not to. But don't worry about it – we've all been there!'

'Amen!' laughed Connor, opening up the door to his

own battered old car and slipping into the driver's seat before the wind could rip it off at the hinges.

'Come on Ivy!' said Rowan, following Connor as she dived into the front passenger seat.

Ivy hesitated for just a second, but then with a quick parting glance at the cow taxi, she darted into the back of Connor's car. It smelled a whole lot nicer than her hire car – there were wafts of engine oil and rusty iron... and something that was just Connor. Kind of Christmassy... and lemony.

Rowan turned and winked at her. 'This more to your taste?' she grinned.

Ivy grinned back.

'Don't worry about Olive,' said Connor, 'I'll explain to her where her car is – and we'll come and collect it and get it back over to the Tallyaff when we get the chance.'

'Yeah, and when the smell won't risk putting us off our Christmas dinner!' added Rowan.

'Are you guys sure Olive won't mind?' said Ivy.

Connor shook his head. 'It's not exactly in great demand at the moment anyway – what with Mr Harris out of action because of his ankle.'

Ivy leaned back in her seat and listened happily as Connor and Rowan started to bicker again. This time, there seemed to be some debate about which route they should take back to the Tallyaff.

'I want to take Ivy to see the standing stones!' said Rowan.

'They're fake!' laughed Connor. 'Mr McCluskey put them up ten years ago for an April fool.'

'Okay fine, misery guts,' huffed Rowan. 'What about the convention centre then?'

'Why on Earth would Ivy want to see that?' said Connor.

'Wait... this place has standing stones *and* a convention centre?' laughed Ivy. 'Is there anything it doesn't have?'

'Ah, you wait for the annual wine festival,' said Connor, 'that's the highlight of the year.'

'Okay, now you're just pulling my leg,' chuckled Ivy. This was all getting more than a little bit bonkers.

'Hey, maybe Ivy would like to see Small Sandy and Loch Crum?' said Rowan.

'I've already seen Big Sandy,' said Ivy.

If she was being honest, what she *really* wanted to do was stop off at Stella's ice cream van on the way back... but she wasn't sure if she should mention it? There'd be no way she'd mention it if she was with Gareth – he'd kick right off about the idea of having ice cream on Christmas morning!

But... she wasn't with Gareth, was she? And if there was one gift she could give herself this Christmas, it was never to hold herself back again just because of what Gareth might think of her... or anyone else, for that matter.

'Any chance we could go and visit the ice cream van?' she said.

'Brilliant idea!' said Rowan, turning to grin at her.

'Perfect - I'm definitely in!' said Connor, reaching out and jamming the radio on.

'Wow now! Two hands on the wheel, you lunatic! I'll DJ' laughed Rowan, as the car veered alarmingly. 'Christmas tunes, big brother?'

'Definitely Christmas tunes!' said Connor.

Rowan fiddled with the dial until a familiar festive tune blasted from the speakers.

Connor thumped his foot onto the accelerator, and within seconds Ivy was grinning as she listened to the brother and sister yelling that they *wished it could be Christmas every daaaaaaaay!* Ivy kept her mouth firmly closed. She couldn't sing for toffee – as she'd proved the previous evening.

'Come on Ivy!' squealed Rowan from the front seat.

Ivy laughed, shrugged, sucked in a lungful of air and joined in at the top of her voice.

It *was* Christmas after all.

CHAPTER 18

❄

'Tub or cone?' asked Stella, grinning at the three of them from the hatch of the cute ice cream van.

'Cone please!' said Ivy, bouncing on her toes in excitement. 'Chocolate orange – two scoops!'

'There's someone who knows how to do Christmas properly!' came a man's voice from behind Stella. A cheery face appeared over her shoulder, grinning happily at Ivy.

'You must be Frank?' said Ivy.

He nodded, sending the bobble of his Christmas hat flapping.

'Sounds like my mum's been waxing lyrical about you again,' laughed Stella, turning to plant a quick kiss on his cheek before starting to serve up Ivy's treat.

'Alright, you two,' said Frank, 'who's having what?'

Connor and Rowan had been arguing about which flavour of ice cream they wanted ever since Ivy had asked if they could stop here on the way back to the Tallyaff – and they were still at it. Frank winked at Ivy and rolled his eyes good-naturedly as he waited for them to decide.

'Okay – I know what I'm having,' said Rowan, her face determined. 'Vanilla, please Frank!'

'Yeah… because she's boring,' said Connor, remaining firmly in naughty six-year-old territory.

Rowan gave him a hefty shove. 'Just because you want something girly,' she said, sticking her tongue out at him.

'I can't help it that strawberry's my favourite!' said Connor.

Ivy took her own loaded cone gratefully from Stella and took a hefty lick.

Mmmmmmm! Christmas in a cone!

Half listening to the other two as they continued to jabber away like two naughty kids, Ivy watched as Stella and Frank manoeuvred around the tiny van interior. It was like watching a perfectly choreographed dance piece. Neither of them seemed to get in the other's way, and they didn't even have to slow down as they went. It was quite something to watch. It was also excruciatingly cute that they pecked each other on the cheek now and then in passing.

'What do I owe you?' Ivy asked once the other two had been firmly silenced by mouthfuls of ice cream

'Get away with you!' laughed Stella. 'It's Christmas Day!'

'That's really kind of you, thanks!' said Ivy.

'What she really means is that she'll add it to your tab at the Tallyaff!' chuckled Connor, his voice thick with strawberry ice cream.

'Don't listen to a word he tells you,' said Stella, rolling her eyes at Connor. 'That boy's been exaggerating ever since we were in primary school!'

Ivy grinned at her. 'Merry Christmas!' she said.

'Merry Christmas!' said Frank. 'We'll see you guys a bit later for lunch at the Tallyaff?'

'Definitely,' said Ivy happily.

Frank pulled the sliding glass of the hatch closed against the chilly gusts of wind that were ruffling the furry brim of his Santa hat. Then the pair of them waved before snuggling in for a cuddle that made Ivy's heart give a twang. That was the kind of love she wanted... but for now, she'd have to make do with ice cream!

Ivy took another huge lick.

'Pretty good, eh?' said Connor, giving her arm a nudge as the three of them headed back towards the shelter of the car.

Ivy nodded. It was easily the best ice cream she'd ever tasted.

'Mr Harris's magic milk, I'm guessing?!' laughed Ivy.

'It's all down to those super-soft hands!' giggled Rowan.

The three of them piled back into Connor's car and finished their cones while the wind did its best to lift them right off their wheels. Ivy sat there, munching away, trying to imagine what it would be like working with someone you loved in such a small space. It must be amazing in that van, listening to the rain beat against the roof and the waves crashing on the nearby shore.

'I'm guessing those two are out in all weathers!' she said. 'They seem pretty happy though.'

'You get used to it here,' said Connor. 'But I'd say those two would be happy practically anywhere, as long as they were together!'

Ivy nodded, though she couldn't really say she knew what that felt like. It certainly wasn't something that she and Gareth had ever managed to achieve. She'd tried to blame her tiny flat for their problems for such a long time – but right now, inside that little ice cream van, Stella and Frank were busily proving her wrong.

The truth was, her and Gareth weren't supposed to share a space together. Share a *life* together. It was as simple as that.

Ivy suddenly knew that she couldn't leave that difficult final conversation with Gareth any longer. She was going to have to do the heartless thing, wasn't she? She was going to have to dump him over the phone on Christmas Day.

❅

CHRISTMAS ON CRUMCAREY

The minute the three of them piled in through the entrance of the Tallyaff, Ivy made her excuses and set off at a run up the stairs. There were two things she needed to do – and she didn't want to give herself time to wimp out. Number one on her list - she needed to call Gareth. Then, number two – she desperately needed that bath!

Ivy grabbed her mobile and went to sit on the bed. This was going to be a difficult enough conversation as it was – so she might as well do it in comfort.

She pulled up Gareth's details and just sat there, staring at them for a moment. Ivy had to admit she was feeling awful about doing this on Christmas Day - but it couldn't be helped. Putting it off was no longer an option. She was already feeling pretty uneasy about the fact that something in her heart seemed to shift every time she looked at Connor.

'Come on, Ivy. Get it over with!' she muttered.

After all, getting dumped by phone on Boxing day wouldn't be much better... or New Year, come to that. Because suddenly Ivy knew for sure that she was no longer in any kind of rush to get back to the mainland.

The moment she pressed the call button, Ivy wished she'd taken a second to figure out what she was going to say!

'What?' Gareth's customary bark made Ivy wince.

'Hi,' she said, her voice uncertain. 'It's me.'

'Good,' said Gareth. 'We need to talk.'

Ivy winced again. She couldn't help it. There wasn't a *Merry Christmas* or even a *hello, how are you?* He was clearly in a foul mood already... and she wasn't about to make it any better, was she?!

'I've been thinking,' said Gareth.

'Me too,' said Ivy.

'About us,' said Gareth.

'Snap,' said Ivy.

'About our future,' said Gareth.

'I know,' sighed Ivy. 'It's like this, I-'

'Will you stop interrupting me?!' snapped Gareth, cutting across her. 'I've got something to say. It's important and it's going to be upsetting, but it needs to be said.'

'O-kay...' said Ivy. This could be interesting. She snuggled back against the pillows and closed her eyes.

'Now that I've had some time on my own, I think we need a break,' said Gareth, his voice coming out in a strange monotone. 'This whole dog thing has brought home to me just how bloody incompatible we are. And then you got on that stupid plane and went off to that stupid island without me - and got *stranded* of all things...' Gareth paused, breathing hard.

Ivy rolled her eyes but didn't say anything.

'You barely even bothered to try to get back here,' he continued, 'even though you knew we had things to discuss. Well - it just shows me how unwilling you are to make the compromises needed for me to be truly happy – in the long term, I mean.'

Ivy raised her eyebrows. This was an awfully long speech for Gareth, and she was getting the sneaking suspicion that he might have it written down in front of him.

'Of course,' he said without waiting for her to speak, 'if you're willing to make the compromises necessary for me to be happy in the long term - and get a dog - ignore everything I've just said.'

Gareth finally stopped talking, but Ivy still didn't say anything. She was sure she'd just heard the rustle of paper on the other end of the line. Hmm - *definitely* a script, then. She'd bet anything that he'd spelt "necessary" wrong, too.

'Well?' prompted Gareth.

'Not really,' said Ivy.

'Not really *what?*' he said, his voice taking on its familiar whining tone.

'I'm not willing to compromise,' said Ivy. 'Not anymore. Not on anything.'

'I thought not,' said Gareth, his voice turning hard. 'That's the thing with selfish people like you.'

Ivy bit her lip. There wasn't much point wasting her breath on him, was there?'

'Obviously,' sighed Gareth, 'this is all going to be very tricky and inconvenient for me. Your flat is close to my work… but I suppose you're going to force me to move out. It might take me a month or two. I think that sounds fair, don't you? I guess I could probably move back in with my parents - I'm sure Mum won't mind.'

Ivy pinched the bridge of her nose hard. The news he wanted to move back in would probably be the worst Christmas present Gareth had ever given his poor mum. The long-suffering woman had probably enjoyed having a couple of years off ironing his underpants!

Not for the first time since arriving on Crumcarey, Ivy wondered how she'd managed to put up with Gareth for so long. Everything had to be about him and about how inconvenient life was for him. This was the Gareth Show, after all.

For a brief moment, Ivy wondered whether she should tell him that she'd met someone else and that she was planning on staying here on Crumcarey for a little while to see how things went. Then she shook her head and almost laughed out loud. Nope – she'd better not! Especially considering she hadn't even breathed a hint of any of this to the "someone else" in question. Poor old Connor!

No, there was no rush. She'd see what happened and try to go with the flow for a change. Of course, she might still end up on the plane back to the mainland the minute it was fixed... but she was willing to throw all plans out of the window and let the winds of Crumcarey decide her fate this time around.

Ivy had the room here at the Tallyaff, and she was prepared to beg Olive to keep it for a few more days... or maybe even weeks if things went well. After all, she could work from anywhere, and she could always ask some of her friends to pack up her most precious possessions and ship them up here for her.

Hmm... she might be getting a *tiny* bit ahead of herself!

'We'll need to discuss dividing our stuff up,' said Gareth, breaking into her thoughts.

'Actually,' said Ivy, her voice now as light as her heart, 'no – we don't.'

She'd already made her choice - she would be staying here on Crumcarey for a while. After that, who knew where her adventure might take her next... maybe she could do a bit of island hopping. One thing was for sure though, she couldn't see herself going back to her flat anytime soon.

'Look,' she said, 'Gareth, why don't you just stay there for now? We can work everything out in the New Year.'

'Oh,' said Gareth. He clearly hadn't been expecting that.

'I'll pay my half of the rent for another month – until I can get my stuff moved out. Then you're on your own,' she said.

'One month is quite short notice to be-' he started.

'The manuals for the toaster, central heating thermostat, cooker, washing machine and all the rest of it are in the left-hand drawer in the kitchen. Second one down - under the tea towels and cutlery,' said Ivy, neatly cutting him off. 'And the iron's in the cupboard under the sink - for your underpants. Merry Christmas!'

With that, she ended the call, hanging up on her past for the last time.

CHAPTER 19

❄

Ivy had just finished drying herself with one of the biggest, fluffiest towels she'd ever had the pleasure of meeting when there was a knock at the door. She quickly wound it around her, tightly wrapping herself up so that she was decent, and then rubbed her face with her hands. She hoped it wasn't too obvious she'd been crying. Weirdly, it wasn't because she was in the least bit upset - it was just from pure relief.

Giving a mighty sniff, she quickly checked herself in the mirror and shrugged. She didn't look too bad - just like she'd overdone things a bit in a super-hot, steamy bath. Crossing her fingers that the towel would stay put and she wasn't about to flash a stranger, she snuck over to the door and cracked it open.

'Olive – hi!' she said in surprise. Her voice came out

a bit squeaky after all that bawling, but if Olive noticed, she had the good grace not to comment on it.

'Ivy dearie!' she said, beaming at her. 'I can't stay long as I'm a bit busy getting everything ready downstairs for dinner, but I thought I'd better pop up and let you know the good news!'

'Good news?' said Ivy, tucking the towel a bit tighter under her armpits.

'Yes!' said Olive with a wide smile. 'Apparently, they're going to send a plane over from the mainland in the morning with some spare parts for Jock. They don't like the idea of us all being cut off with no transport while we wait for poor Connor to sort out the ferry. So they've said they're happy for you to catch a lift back to the mainland when they return! You'll be able to get back to your fiancé at last – I'm just sorry it's taken so long!'

'Oh,' said Ivy, the smile tumbling from her face no matter how hard she tried to hitch it back in place. 'Oh,' she said again, this time it came out as a whisper. 'A lift back. Right.'

'What is it, dearie?' said Olive in evident concern. 'I thought you'd be happy!'

'I've just split up with Gareth,' said Ivy.

'Oh,' said Olive, her hand shooting out to pat Ivy on the shoulder. 'Oh, my love, I'm so sorry. What awful news… and on Christmas Day too.'

'It's fine,' said Ivy, letting out a sound that was half a laugh and half a sob. 'Really. It's actually a huge relief.'

'Oh,' said Olive again, now looking decidedly confused. 'Well... at least you can still leave Crumcarey in the morning and head back to your friends for a bit of TLC.'

'Actually,' said Ivy, rubbing her eyes, irritated with herself for being so ridiculous, 'I was wondering if you'd be willing to let me have the room for a bit longer? I was hoping I might be able... to stay?'

'Stay?' said Olive, her eyebrows shooting up into her hairline.

Ivy smiled at her and nodded. It was obvious that it took some doing to take Olive Martinelli by surprise, but she had a sneaking suspicion that she might have just managed it!

'You're going to have to tell me everything – and I *mean* everything!' said Olive, looking intrigued. 'But... not now. I've really got to get back downstairs!'

'I promise!' laughed Ivy. 'It's quite a long story! But... if I can stay here a bit longer, that would be amazing?'

'Of course! The room's yours as long as you need it,' said Olive. 'This wouldn't have anything to do with a certain handsome Connor-shaped person, would it?'

Her blush was so sudden that Ivy wouldn't be surprised if it was making her damp hair steam. But then... it was clear not much got past Olive. Besides... she had a daughter of her own who was currently cuddled up in a freezing-cold ice cream van down on the dunes. She'd probably had plenty of practice recognising the signs!

'Might do,' muttered Ivy, shooting her a quick smile. 'I think it's a bit early to say, though.'

'So... how long were you planning on staying?' said Olive lightly.

'Oh,' said Ivy, 'I'm not really sure... as long as it takes, I guess.'

'That's my girl,' said Olive, giving her an approving nod. 'It's a good thing I booked your place for Christmas dinner too, isn't it?'

Ivy nodded. 'You're my hero.'

'Aw – get away with you!' chuckled Olive. 'You're on the same table as Connor and Rowan - I hope that's alright with you?'

'That sounds just about perfect,' said Ivy, as her heart did an excited backflip. 'Thanks!'

Olive started to pull the door closed but then turned back to Ivy.

'I almost forgot, I've got this for you!' She drew out a gold-wrapped parcel from behind her back and handed it over.

'What's this?' said Ivy in surprise.

'It *is* Christmas, love,' laughed Olive, 'it's a present!'

'But I haven't got anything for you!' said Ivy.

'Well, dear,' said Olive. 'This is from the whole of Crumcarey, not just me. And anyway, just yesterday, you didn't even know me so I don't think you need to worry about Christmas presents this time around. Maybe next year, eh?!'

Ivy gaped at Olive for a moment. Had it really only been yesterday that she'd arrived? Hell – just yesterday morning, she hadn't even met Connor, and now she was seriously considering turning her entire life upside down for him. In fact, she'd already turned her entire life upside down... but that bit hadn't been for him. That had been for her.

'Well, I'll leave you to it,' said Olive. 'I hope you like your Christmas present. I would suggest that maybe you pop it on before you come down for lunch.'

'Pop it on?' said Ivy.

'You'll know what I mean when you open it,' said Olive. 'Now I've got to get back down to the kitchen before those spr-carrots are boiled to a mush.'

'Nothing worse than a mushy carrot!' said Ivy, grinning at Olive before she finally disappeared.

Ivy took the present back over to the bed and flopped down for a moment. As excited as she was to get back downstairs and join in the fun with Connor and Rowan, she needed a couple more minutes to herself to let everything sink in a bit.

A wave of bone-deep tiredness swept over her, and for a second, she had to fight the urge not to scramble underneath the blanket for a quick snooze... but she didn't dare – she'd probably be asleep until New Year if she did that.

Besides, she needed to get a wiggle on and tidy

herself up a bit before going back downstairs to face what sounded like most of the population of Crumcarey... that's if the babble of cheerful voices drifting up through the floorboards was anything to go by.

Ivy had already lounged around in the glorious bathtub while she'd sobbed in relief at finally being free of Gareth. The hot water had been blissful, and Olive's carefully selected toiletries were just as yummy as she'd dreamed they'd be. At least it meant she smelled a lot nicer than she had in a very long time! Unfortunately the same couldn't be said for her clothes.

Urgh – she hated the idea of going downstairs in the same things she'd been wearing when she'd arrived on the island! Ah well, she'd worry about that in a moment. First things first – it was time to open her one and only Christmas present. She pulled the beautifully wrapped gold parcel towards her and tugged on the pretty piece of ribbon. Ivy carefully peeled off layers of tissue paper to reveal something soft, in a striking red tartan.

Ivy plucked it out of the bed of tissue and gave it a shake. It looked to be the bottom half of a pair of pyjamas. She quickly grabbed the second item and grinned as she unfolded it. It was a long-sleeved, flannel top with *Welcome to Crumcarey* embroidered right across the front. Ivy let out a surprised laugh. Well – at least that solved the problem of what she was going to wear for Christmas lunch. As Olive had been the one to tell her to "pop it on", she didn't need to worry about whether rocking up to lunch in a pair of PJs might offend anyone.

Ivy ran her fingers through her hair and quickly pulled it back into two plaits. It wasn't much, but at least it was clean and tidy. She wished more than anything that she had her toiletries case with her – but all she'd brought to Crumcarey was her little travel handbag. Still – there might be something useful somewhere in its depths!

After ferreting around for a minute, Ivy triumphantly pulled out a mascara she'd popped in there last summer when she'd gone to her best friend's wedding, along with a little pot of Vaseline. Ivy knew that no one here really cared what she looked like, but it would be nice to face Connor not feeling like she'd just been trampled by Mr Harris's herd!

Now all she had to do was make sure she didn't decide to treat Crumcarey to any more of her *very special* singing or dancing over dinner! She'd done enough of that the previous evening. Ivy wrinkled her nose. There was a small part of her that was dreading showing her face after last night. She might not be able to remember much about the crowd she'd entertained, but little snatches of laughing and cheering kept surfacing in her memory.

Ah well, now wasn't the time to get cold feet was it? Besides, everyone she'd met on Crumcarey so far had been... different. Here. people's default settings seemed to be stuck on "kind". She felt free and more alive than she had done in years. Almost two years, to be precise.

Ivy brushed her hands over her brand-new pyjamas and let out a happy sigh. She quickly pulled on her socks and trainers and glanced at herself in the mirror. Yeah, she definitely looked a bit odd, but somehow it just didn't matter. Though... if she really was going to stay longer, she was going to have to beg Olive to let her wash and dry her clothes! Or, maybe she could make a quick dash over to the motel to grab her case... maybe Connor would take her.

Today felt like it could be the beginning of something special. And everything that had happened so far had led up to it, including the weird bits. It was definitely time to embrace the weird, the wonderful and anything else life decided to throw at her!

Ivy had always tried to stay in control – she'd always been Miss Five-Year Plan. But look where that had got her. She was ready for an adventure for the first time in her life... No plans. No definites... other than the fact that there was a man downstairs that had the ability to turn her knees to jelly with just one look.

CHAPTER 20

Ivy paused at the bottom of the stairs. Her heart was thumping and her palms were sweating. She couldn't believe how nervous she was... and the roar of excited voices coming from the direction of the bar wasn't helping matters much.

It had been such a lovely morning, and her time with Rowan and Connor had been surprisingly easygoing... but now? She wasn't so sure. Ivy took a deep breath. She was being ridiculous. There was no pressure. No expectation. No need to do anything other than enjoy spending more time with her new friends while mainlining as much turkey as was humanly possible.

Striding forward before she could change her mind again, Ivy pushed on the door that led through to the bar. She was greeted by a wall of chattering, happy voices underscored by the gorgeous crooning of old-fashioned Christmas tunes coming from a gramophone that had been set up on the bar.

The entire room had been transformed in the relatively short time Ivy had been upstairs. Glittering garlands looped from the ceiling, and below them, the room was now full of tables. Crammed in around them were dozens of excited, happy faces - all ready to tuck into their Christmas dinner. In fact, it looked like she was probably one of the last to be seated.

The Tallyaff was absolutely packed. Ivy quickly scanned the crowd, looking for Rowan and Connor. At last, she spotted her empty seat at their table over near the wood burner.

Feeling suddenly shy, Ivy dropped her eyes and started to make her way through the throng, picking her way between the tables that had been packed in like sardines.

'Merry Christmas, Ivy!'

Ivy peeped up, only to come face to face with Mr Harris.

'Merry Christmas!' she replied.

'I hope you're going to give us a song or two later,' he said, grinning at her.

'Erm... I'll do my best *not* to!' she replied, returning his smile.

'You enjoy your lunch now, my girl!' he said, giving her a quick wink.

'You too... and McGregor!' she added, noticing the little dog sitting patiently under the old man's chair.

As she carried on over towards her empty seat, Ivy picked out a few more faces that she knew in the crowd. There was Jock, the pilot who'd flown her over to Crumcarey, sitting at the same table as Frank and Stella.

Ivy soon found it didn't matter whether she knew people or not, every single person she passed had a friendly greeting for her or a cheeky comment about her singing. Strangely – the cheekier they got, the more Ivy relaxed. Suddenly, she felt like she'd been part of this tight-knit community for years, rather than just hours!

At long last, she reached the spot where Rowan and Connor were waiting for her and sank gratefully into her chair.

'Sorry I took so long,' she muttered.

'Ha!' said Rowan, giving her a one-armed squeeze. 'I'm kind of glad you did – that was like watching a walk of shame on steroids! I'm so gutted I missed your performance last night.'

'Leave her be!' muttered Connor, smiling at Ivy.

'Don't be a killjoy,' chuckled Rowan. 'I must be the only person on Crumcarey who missed it!'

'Well… ply me with plenty of Olive's whiskey collection and you might get an encore one day,' said Ivy, grinning at Rowan.

At that moment, Olive appeared from the kitchen bearing the biggest plate of roast turkey Ivy had ever seen. She was promptly greeted by a wave of clapping and cheering, and Ivy joined in with gusto. Her mouth started to water as Olive's husband and various helpers followed with a line-up of roast potatoes, assorted veg and, of course, a towering pan of brussels sprouts – which was greeted by a resounding cheer of "bring oot the carrots!"

As the mammoth task of serving up started, Ivy watched Connor. She was bursting to talk to him, and as soon as Rowan was distracted by a woman at the next table passing over a bowl of stuffing balls, she took her chance.

Leaning forwards, she whispered in Connor's ear.

'I'm staying,' she said. 'On Crumcarey!' she added, just in case there was any confusion.

'I know,' said Connor, looking at her in amusement. 'Olive just told me.'

Of course she did! Ivy shook her head. The island grapevine was clearly good and strong... and ridiculously fast, too!

'And?' she asked, her heart thumping with nerves.

She wasn't really sure what she was expecting him to say. After all, she'd only met the poor guy yesterday. Since then, she'd managed to cause absolute havoc. She'd woken him up with her appalling singing, declared whiskey-fuelled love on the stairs, and then forced him to spend last night keeping half an eye that she didn't choke on her own vomit.

Nice!

Then, of course, she'd ruined his Christmas morning too.

Only... she hadn't ruined it, had she? She, Connor and Rowan had spent a lovely morning together. But still, she had no idea what he was going to say about the fact that she'd decided to stay.

'What do you think?' she prompted quietly.

Connor stared at her for a few moments and then, out of the blue, he leaned forward. Very purposefully, he tilted her chin up with his fingers and pulled her in for a long, slow kiss.

Another huge round of applause and whistling broke out, echoing from all four corners of the room.

When Connor eventually drew away from her, Ivy's face was both beaming and boiling in equal measure. She caught sight of Rowan over Connor's shoulder, busy clapping and cheering with everyone else.

'I thought you were leaving,' said Connor. 'Otherwise, I would have done that a lot sooner.'

'I call bullshit,' said Rowan. 'You were just sulking because you thought she belonged to someone else. He's been dying to do that all morning – ever since you let slip that you aren't engaged!'

Connor leaned over and ruffled Rowan's hair in an attempt to shut her up, and she promptly retaliated by pulling his Christmas hat down over his eyes so that he couldn't see.

'I'm just saying – he'd have snogged your face off whether you were planning to leave or not!' said

Rowan hastily, before Connor reached out and pushed her clean off her chair.

Ivy, who felt like her entire world had just spun on its axis, watched them bickering with a dazed grin on her face. In a way, she was glad that it was far too manic in here right now to discuss what had just happened.

Suddenly, plates and cutlery were being handed around, followed by serving bowls full of stuffing and sausages to deal with. Next came huge vats of gravy and bottle after bottle of wine. Everything else was forgotten while the food and drink came thick and fast.

Tucking into her delicious meal, Ivy almost choked on her pig-in-a-blanket when someone started to play footsie with her under the table. She stared at Connor, raising her eyebrows in amused delight. Connor, however, was busy digging into his meal and didn't seem to notice.

There it was again!

'Hey!' she laughed, shooting him a cheeky little wink when he finally looked up.

'What?' said Connor, almost choking on a parsnip.

'What do you mean *what?!*' said Ivy.

'Yeah, *what* Conor?' said Rowan.

There it was again – a little sly nudge of her foot. What on Earth was going on? She peered under the table, determined to find out, only to find McGregor staring back at her - his little doggie eyes pleading and sorrowful.

Oh God, she'd just been playing footsie with the dog, hadn't she? She glanced up only to meet Rowan's naughty, twinkling eyes.

'Making new friends?' she said innocently.

Ivy stuck her tongue out at Rowan, making Connor chuckle. She leaned down to give McGregor a little tickle behind the ears before offering him a bit of sausage.

She had about two seconds to wonder if this was such a good idea – after all, the dog did have a bad reputation! But McGregor took the piece of sausage as gently as a little lamb. He gulped it down without even chewing it, gave her hand a grateful lick, and wandered over to the next table to see if he could work the same trick on them.

'Little scam artist!' laughed Ivy.

'You wait,' said Connor, 'he'll be back around again!'

Ivy grinned and glanced around the room. It was lovely to see so many happy faces tucking into their Christmas meal. Mr Harris was leaning over his plate as if he was protecting it, eating with his elbows out to ward off any competition. No wonder McGregor was on the scrounge – it didn't look like he had any hope of getting a treat off his master's plate!

After she'd finished stuffing her face, Ivy leaned back in her chair with a satisfied little groan. She wished she had more room for seconds or thirds… or whatever helping she was on by this point… but she was officially full. Then again, she might just manage to fit some pudding in after she'd had a couple of minutes to re-group.

Ivy closed her eyes and let the warm babble of Christmas chatter wash over her. As a gentle hymn crackled from the gramophone, she felt fingers twining with hers under the table. Smiling, she opened her eyes… just to check… but this time it *was* Connor.

She stared at their clasped hands for a moment, then at Connor, and then over towards Stella and Frank. Their love had brought them all the way from Devon to Crumcarey. Maybe this was Ivy's chance to find her own love story. As Connor's thumb started to trace tingling patterns across her hand, she couldn't help but think that she was in with a chance… a very good chance.

'You know,' said Connor quietly into her ear. 'I'm not telling Rowan she's right… but I wanted to kiss you from the moment I set eyes on you.'

'Really?' said Ivy with a little laugh. 'You mean when I was doing a drowned rat impression? And you were delirious from working for twenty-nine hours straight, on the biggest coffee-high of your entire life, and covered in grease while a boat engine dangled over your head?'

'I thought you liked me covered in grease?' said Connor.

So, he'd noticed the fact that she'd been unable to take her eyes off him the entire time?!

'You know,' he laughed, 'I have to say - you smell a

lot better than you did earlier! Plus, you look incredibly cute in these,' he added, tweaking the collar of her pyjamas. 'So... can I kiss you again?'

'Witter woo!' cheered Rowan half-heartedly. She was sitting with her eyes closed, cradling her full stomach with her hands – though she clearly couldn't bear to let a chance of annoying her big brother pass her by.

'Maybe not in front of the entire island this time?' chuckled Ivy.

'Do you really care?' said Conor.

'Not in the slightest,' said Ivy, leaning forward and reaching out to drag him closer.

This time there was just a little wave of giggling that travelled around the room. This sort of thing clearly happened quite a lot on Crumcarey when the wine started flowing and the food was this good.

Pulling back, Ivy squeezed Connor's hand and let out a contented sigh. She had a whole island to explore, actually - three islands if you counted The Dot and Little Crum. She'd come all this way on an unexpected adventure – and somehow it felt like it was only just getting going.

Who would have thought that *not* getting a dog could have changed her life so much? Not that getting the dog was a bad idea in itself. Maybe one day they could get one a little bit like McGregor. Then again, perhaps that was a conversation to have with Connor at a later date. A much, *much* later date!

Ivy looked around as everyone started to chink their glasses, only to spot Olive getting to her feet and raising her glass.

'Merry Christmas everyone,' she beamed, 'and a happy New Year!'

You bet! thought Ivy, cheering with everyone else as she locked eyes with Connor again. Suddenly, life felt rather wonderful.

Connor was wonderful.

Crumcarey was wonderful.

Uh oh! If she didn't watch out, she was going to start singing again!

THE END

ALSO BY BETH RAIN

Little Bamton Series:

Little Bamton: The Complete Series Collection: Books 1 - 5

Individual titles:

Christmas Lights and Snowball Fights (Little Bamton Book 1)

Spring Flowers and April Showers (Little Bamton Book 2)

Summer Nights and Pillow Fights (Little Bamton Book 3)

Autumn Cuddles and Muddy Puddles (Little Bamton Book 4)

Christmas Flings and Wedding Rings (Little Bamton Book 5)

Upper Bamton Series:

A New Arrival in Upper Bamton (Upper Bamton Book 1)

Rainy Days in Upper Bamton (Upper Bamton Book 2)

Hidden Treasures in Upper Bamton (Upper Bamton Book 3)

Time Flies By in Upper Bamton (Upper Bamton Book 4)

Seabury Series:

Welcome to Seabury (Seabury Book 1)

Trouble in Seabury (Seabury Book 2)

Christmas in Seabury (Seabury Book 3)

Sandwiches in Seabury (Seabury Book 4)

Secrets in Seabury (Seabury Book 5)

Surprises in Seabury (Seabury Book 6)

Dreams and Ice Creams in Seabury (Seabury Book 7)

Mistakes and Heartbreaks in Seabury (Seabury Book 8)

Laughter and Happy Ever After in Seabury (Seabury Book 9)

Seabury Series Collections:

Kate's Story: Books 1 - 3

Hattie's Story: Books 4 - 6

Writing as Bea Fox:

What's a Girl To Do? The Complete Series

Individual titles:

The Holiday: What's a Girl To Do? (Book 1)

The Wedding: What's a Girl To Do? (Book 2)

The Lookalike: What's a Girl To Do? (Book 3)

The Reunion: What's a Girl To Do? (Book 4)

At Christmas: What's a Girl To Do? (Book 5)

ABOUT THE AUTHOR

Beth Rain has always wanted to be a writer and has been penning adventures for characters ever since she learned to stare into the middle-distance and daydream.

She currently lives in the (sometimes) sunny South West, and it is a dream come true to spend her days hanging out with Bob – her trusty laptop – scoffing crisps and chocolate while dreaming up swoony love stories for all her imaginary friends.

Beth's writing will always deliver on the happy-ever-afters, so if you need cosy… you're in safe hands!

Visit www.bethrain.com for all the bookish goodness and keep up with all Beth's news by joining her monthly newsletter!

facebook.com/BethRainBooks
twitter.com/bethrainauthor
instagram.com/bethrainauthor

Printed in Great Britain
by Amazon